Mills & Boon
Best Seller Romance

A chance to read and collect some of the best-loved novels from Mills & Boon—the world's largest publisher of romantic fiction.

Every month, six titles by favourite Mills & Boon authors will be re-published in the *Best Seller Romance* series.

A list of other titles in the *Best Seller Romance* series can be found at the end of this book.

Margaret Way

NOONFIRE

MILLS & BOON LIMITED
LONDON · TORONTO

First published 1972
Australian copyright 1983
Philippine copyright 1983
This edition 1983

© Margaret Way 1972 ✗

ISBN 0 263 74392 6

Set in Linotype Plantin 11 on 11½ pt.
02 – 0883

Made and printed in Great Britain by Richard Clay (The Chaucer Press) Ltd, Bungay, Suffolk

CHAPTER ONE

IT rained the day of the funeral; a day to end all days; the skies leaden, the wind, rain-driven, and when she got home she was chilled to the bone, wisps of the service clinging to her like some eerie mist; the cold, bleak church, the mellifluous flow of the minister's voice, by-passed by personal grief . . . the frailty of life, the inevitability of its end, the resurrection and the life . . . pitched to a sombre note but delivered with perfect self-assurance, broken by spasmodic jangles as a door opened, letting in the outside roar of the traffic, the sudden murmured little breaths of sympathy that came in soft jolts against her ear, to shock her out of her unsharable melancholy. The whole scene played out through a dark veil, shot by an odd sense of unreality under which her composure wavered and trembled but never broke.

The rain was still falling in metallic grey sheets as she let herself into the house, shrugging out of her wet things. She sank against the front door, unutterably sick and fatigued. Now at last, tears burned out of the sides of her eyes sliding weakly along her pale cheeks, making it difficult for her to see. Her head was thrown back, tilted upwards towards the shadowy, shimmering stairway that spiralled into the first floor. Then, without the slightest change of expression, she went towards it, pulling herself upwards, holding on to the baluster as if to save herself from falling.

The door to her mother's room lay open. The room itself, austerely elegant and fastidious, the windows shuttered in a kind of ceremonial dignity. Death had

5

been due to natural causes, specifically coronary throm-
bosis brought on by an emotional disturbance. One in
countless emotional dramas that had played themselves
out since Rory's earliest childhood. Unconsciously her
head was braced, her young face showing every indication of strain, her mind fine-tuned to her 'voices'.

'But you *can't*, Rory! You must not!'

'But why not, Mother?'

The words careered at her, echoing out of a ringing
void. The voice was perplexed, innocent, a questioning
child's. Coming again, stronger this time, firming with
approaching maturity:

'But you must have a *better* reason, surely,
Mother?'

'I absolutely *forbid* it!'

The answering voice was abysmally bitter, the face
cold and set, before it dissolved and crumpled into hys-
terical tears. In a sudden breathless rush Rory lurched
forward and clutched at a delicate, brocade-covered
chair, sank into it and put her head down. Nausea began
to mount in her, but she held it down, knowing that she
would give away entirely if she allowed this sickness to
grow. It was no more than a fainting spell brought about
by hunger and exhaustion, the overlying deep sense of
grief and melancholia for what might have been.

When she had changed her clothes she would have to
eat something. Perhaps she could manage a cup of
coffee and a sandwich. Choke it down somehow, for she
had to keep going at all costs. But *did* she? Was it worth
the effort? Was *anything* worth troubling about? Gradually calm returned to her features, cold reason to her
mind. The house would have to go. She could never
maintain it on her own and Kim would never live in it.
'Old Mausolus's tomb!' he had irreverently dubbed it,

in the very early days, but never within earshot of her mother, for obscurely her mother had allowed her friendship with Kim Barrett to continue, fostering it for once, without opposition.

Kim Barrett was blond and moderately good-looking; of good family, but best of all, steady and reliable. Already in his mid-twenties, he was very well placed in the bank where he worked and he was ambitious, charmingly deferential to those older and wiser, like her mother. For over a year now his interest in Rory Sheridan had been all-exclusive, but he had missed the funeral at a time when Rory could have done with his support.

The sickness and the dizziness had passed. Rory stood up with a carefully cultivated serenity and walked along the corridor to her own bedroom. It was much smaller than her mother's, lacking its handsome furnishings, but it shared a compartmented bathroom with the master bedroom. The decor was cool and restful with a subtle grey and white toile on the walls, touches of colour here and there of pure, clear green in the cushions and side drapes, a lacy white canopy over the Colonial iron and brass bed she had unearthed in a junk shop and spent loving hours labouring on its restoration. The overmantel watercolour was her own, a landscape, a personal impression of the river and gum trees touched by a golden shower of late afternoon light, for her bedroom had long doubled as a secluded study; a retreat and a haven when household tensions mounted to agitation point.

But now the seemingly unalterable pattern of her life had changed. Her mother had gone and she faced life on her own, the survivor of many lone battles, facing a future she didn't seem to want. Her head was bowed, her face washed clear of emotion as though the events of the day had utterly defeated her, then suddenly she

7

jerked up her head and walked across to her dressing-table, slid open a drawer and took from it a long flat box covered in olive green velvet. Her fingers curved around the box, shaking slightly, then she opened it.

The pearls lay gleaming, softly lustrous, the treasures of the Coral Seas. The fine diamond clasp glittered impersonally, rayed with blue light. They had arrived in time for her eighteenth birthday and it had taken a scene to keep them. The matching earrings, circled by diamonds, arrived a year later. No scene this time, only an icy displeasure, a moody embittered silence that lasted for days.

Rory put the box down and walked across to the wardrobe, reaching for a small suitcase shoved out of sight in its deepest recesses. Her hand fastened on a strap and she drew it out on to the carpet. It had a musty neglected look after its long, enforced storage. She unbuckled the straps and threw open the lid. Even now she couldn't control an overwhelming sense of guilt and defiance as she looked down at its contents, although her mother was no longer there to be distressed by them. It was almost beyond her comprehension to realize her mother was forever free of all the old heartaches. She could almost hear her moving about in the next room. She dug her teeth into her trembling lip and tasted blood in her mouth. Her eyes, glittery with tears, rested on a small Polynesian idol that grinned back at her grotesquely. She picked it up and cradled it in her palm.

There were others; carvings of all kinds and artifacts; some aboriginal, some collected from voyages all over the South Seas; a lovely gold lip pearl shell from Torres Strait packed in cotton wool, a glistening stuffed baby crocodile, the man-eating variety from the Adelaide River outside Darwin; a bottle full of amethysts and other gemstones, another of opals from Coober

8

Pedy, the chalk white inland sea of prehistory.

Under her misted vision, the opals flashed out their milky locked message; blue, gold and purple, bright streaks of crimson and green. Her father had sent all of them, but in a sense, she had won all these small treasures for herself. The others, the dolls and the books and the clothes, the *muu-muus*, the *pareus* and the grass skirts had found their way into the incinerator close on arrival while the small girl, Rory, stood breathless but tearless, imagining their fiery destruction, as distressed in her way as her mother undoubtedly was on the isolated occasions when the gifts arrived.

When her father finally tired of the adventuring, the Pacific-bound wanderings that had driven her mother into leaving him when Rory was barely four, he had settled in North Queensland, buying into a sugar plantation. The divorce had gone through by then and her father's name became the unspeakable word. But from then on, ironically, the money poured in. By some perverse turn of fortune, everything Bren Sheridan touched brought forth a golden shower of profits. One highly successful financial operation followed another, so that barely a decade later, a thousand miles away in the State Capital, Sheridan Enterprises was synonymous with a gilt-edged investment.

Bren Sheridan had a finger in the North's every big venture – sugar, beef, mining, real estate, even the prawning wealth of the Gulf. When Rory was twelve, he had committed the unforgivable, the damning, the ultimate sin. He had remarried; an Italian woman, a beauty by all accounts, a widow with two children of her own. Rory could remember as clearly as if it were yesterday the tirade that event had called forth. That was the time she began wishing herself a small bird who could fly the scene of those short dreadful outbursts.

9

Her father was a rogue and a scoundrel, a man who had wrecked every chance of happiness Sara Sheridan had had in life, the irreplaceable privileges that went with a home and a man of one's own, the loving family unit. There was not a man in the world to be trusted. They were all fools or villains, the lot of them. Not *one* worth the love of a good woman. *And* the woman – an Italian, a foreigner! Not content with having had one man she must needs collect two as her due. If there was anything even remotely ludicrous about the whole situation neither Rory nor her mother saw it, both in their own way suffering.

Yet her father continued to maintain them, and maintain them in style. Rory had gone to the best schools. Their house, never a home, was in a fashionable neighbourhood and her mother, consciously or unconsciously, had developed over the years a compensating taste for quiet luxury. In the years of his success, Brendan Sheridan had denied them no material advantage, but Rory had never laid eyes on him since the day her mother had bundled her into a few clothes, snatched up all the available money she could find and boarded a plane, as far away from the man she had once loved as she could get.

Rory couldn't remember her father, though her imagination had built up a complete portrait that was in no way authenticated in life, rather a composite picture of the loving and devoted fathers who came to school functions so obviously proud of their wives, their daughters' accomplishments. Rory had done extremely well at school, driven back on herself into long hours of study, but only on rare occasions did her mother attend prize-givings and only then when her indifferent health permitted. And so life continued with each slipping back into their separate identities, for Rory in no way resembled her mother. But her mother had *loved* her. She was sure of that. Only that love and life itself had been flawed by a deep-driven resentment, a railing at fate, a humiliated pride that gave her no peace. Always and forever, Sara Sheridan had been bitterly conscious of being a woman on her own, with no man at her shoulder, regarding this unswervingly as a personal affront, believing to the end that she had taken the only possible course open to her in severing her own marriage.

So much a product of her environment, Rory had grown up a lonely and alone child, showing to the world only what she wished them to see, keeping her multiple small miseries to herself, earning for herself the reputation for being a gifted but aloof child when all she wanted was what other girls accepted as naturally as the air they breathed; a loving and stable home atmosphere, a family unit, united and secure; brothers and sisters to fight and have fun with, to range alongside, an indivisible team when one of their number was threatened in even the slightest way.

Her father had sent an enormous sheaf of orchids and white ginger blossom to the funeral. In the early days of their marriage Sara Sheridan had surrounded herself with both, exotic compensations for life in the tropics. The heavy, sweet scent of the ginger blossom seemed to cling to her dress. Rory got up from her knees swaying a little. Did anything bear thinking about? Once two people had loved each other. She had been born of that brief, stormy union. Her mother had made her agonizing decision and suffered long for it. Now it was too late for anything. Failure all along the line, the tumult and chaos of an unhappy marriage. They were only the broad outlines revealing nothing of the day-to-day frustrations. One couldn't readily picture her mother against a laughing happy background. She fitted too well the peculiar intensity of the role she had played. Wanting too much, understanding too little, she had made her own private hell and unwittingly not wanting it, had drawn a small child into it. But feeling between mother and child, however strained and precarious, could never be completely blotted out. Her mother's griefs had been her own and always in the end she had said or done instinctively what was wisest and best, for Rory, even as a child, provided a balance for her mother's temperament, living through the days of crashing tension when her mother seemed to brood endlessly over the old disasters. Even now she could recall vividly the sensation of oppression, of adult mistakes bearing down on her though she didn't know it at the time. A single, carefree day with no cloud on the horizon was almost totally strange to her, though that fact too she only gradually awakened to.

The phone suddenly shrilled on the upstairs extension, cutting cruelly across her ragged nerves. She retraced her steps to her mother's bedroom and lifted the receiver. The voice at the other end didn't wait for an acknowledgment but spoke directly into the void:

'Rory darling, is that you?'

She bit on her lip at that friendly, familiar voice, threaded with anxiety. 'Yes, Kim. I missed you!' There was no trace of irony in her voice but a simple statement of fact.

'I know, darling. You've no idea how I tried, but old Harris is a callous swine at the best of times. He wanted a certain report and that was that, but I thought of you incessantly all through the afternoon. I'll come round now, shall I? I can't bear the thought of your brooding in that old barn on your own. Give me twenty minutes.'

'No, don't, Kim!' Suddenly for no good reason it

seemed the most desirable thing in the world to be on her own. 'I have a frightful headache. I'll turn in early. Don't worry. I'm quite all right!'

'But are you, darling? How can I be sure of that? You keep so much to yourself. That reserve of yours, sweetheart, is the very devil!'

'Please, Kim!'

'Oh, very well, if you insist, but I'm not at all sure I'm doing the right thing. I'll call in tomorrow on my way to work. Good night, my love!'

'Good night, Kim!' She hung up with finality, strangely uncomforted, not really certain in that moment of her exact feelings towards Kim Barrett. She only knew he had become part of her lonely existence, physically attractive yet undemanding, intelligent and well informed and the enviable recipient of her mother's favour. Other young men before him, more sharply individual, had not been nearly so fortunate, and fared badly in the cold war her mother could wage to perfection.

Rory walked back along the hallway, unzipping her black wool frock as she went, pulling it over her head and throwing it down on the bed where it spilled in a heap, starkly ominous against the woven white bedspread. A fold of her robe gleamed from the open door of her wardrobe and she reached for it abstractedly, slipping her arms into the long sleeves and knotting the silken cord around her narrow waist. Her head was aching abominably. She pulled at the pins that secured her hair in its customary neat knot at her nape and let it fall in a thick, heavy swathe against her face. It was relief of a kind and it altered the composition of her face in an arresting fashion, but she never noticed it herself.

Later she carried a cup of coffee into the living-room

and settled back in her favourite wing-backed chair. So physically and mentally exhausted was she that she began to experience a sensation almost of calm, an indifference to everything. It was growing dark, but she didn't bother to turn on a light. She just continued to sit in a state of suspended cerebration where nothing had any real meaning and only night and sleep would seal off this curious vacuum in which she found herself. Even now she could smell the white ginger blossom, a fragrance on her very skin. How strange! Yet it was forever to be trapped in her senses.

What kind of man was her father? According to her mother he was selfish and self-orientated, incredibly irresponsible as a young man with considerable charm but little real integrity, a man whose passion for all sorts of dangerous adventures had left her repelled. A man whose every word had been barbed, double-edged, a weapon to wound. Knowing how easy it had been to wound her mother, Rory had reason to temper this harsh judgment. Yet her father had never sent for her, never expressed a desire to see her beyond a one and only request for access sent through his solicitors, which brought on her mother's first real 'attack' while the child Rory cried and stormed and told her mother's doctor she never, *never* wanted to be with her father, for he was a *bad* man. There were no more requests after that.

How long she sat there, Rory never knew. She got up once to switch on a few lights, then sat down again. She might almost have been drifting on the borderline of sleep when the front door bell rang, bringing her back to her senses. She sprang up with an agitated little movement, her hand going to her tumbled hair, then to the neck of her robe, as if mentally squaring her shoulders with the gesture. She went out to the hallway and switched on the small chandelier that threw a pool of light over the front door and the darkness beyond.

It was Kim, his good-looking face, demanding reassurance, sharp with concern.

'I know you said not to, but I couldn't help myself. Let me in, darling!'

She stood back without a word, heedless of the chill wind blowing, almost bereft of speech, delayed shock deadening her impulses. He put his hand over her nerveless fingers and shut the door with a soft thud, then took her into his arms, not kissing her, feeling the living warmth and scent of her.

'Rory darling!'

It was the devil's own job holding himself back, but it was an art he had acquired in the very early stages of their friendship — not without considerable misgiving. Rory Sheridan, he had discovered, was cool to the point of coldness, responding to only the most restrained lovemaking, yet awareness brought the accompanying familiar sense of frustration. He knew he had to respect her depths of reserve, her grief for her mother. For himself, however, it was impossible to feel anything beyond a certain sense of release, believing as he did that Sara Sheridan had been her own and her daughter's worst enemy, a face-to-face unpalatable fact. He could have attended the funeral if he had tried hard enough, but on his own reckoning it would have amounted to a form of hypocrisy. That he had tried hard enough to win and retain Sara Sheridan's approval during life was now characteristically forgotten. With her mother gone, he could expect Rory to come alive, react as she should, for her control seemed unnatural to him for a girl of twenty.

He held her away from him, allowing his eyes to rest on her, studying every detail of her appearance. It had always seemed to him from the moment of their meeting that Rory Sheridan was quite something, though she went out of her way to play her looks down – but now suddenly she was disturbingly beautiful. Despite her extreme pallor, her eyes reflected the jade green of her quilted satin robe, startlingly clear under their slanting dark brows, the iris unflecked by any other colour, the only points of brilliance in the pale oval of her face.

It was hard to pinpoint the exact difference in her appearance unless it was the lovely, innocent allure of her slender young body in its soft wrap or the heavy sweep of her dark auburn hair falling loose against creamy skin when she always dressed it so severely. Strange, he mused, that her manner should be so at odds with her appearance; the warmth of her colouring, the shape of her eyes, the curve of her mouth, the slant of her brows, the unconscious promise that was held so rigidly under restraint.

Imagining him a past master in the art of persuasion, Rory Sheridan still held herself aloof from him, her fascination surviving in the strangest way, this new vulnerability, the haunting, forlorn look in the depths of her eyes, oddly exciting. At last he stopped looking at her, realizing that it was out of keeping with his carefully maintained manner. Individual privacy was something she prized. He hadn't cared to comprehend it at first, but the fact was soon driven home on him. He saw her wide, black-lashed eyes waver uncertainly and he released her and turned her gently into the living-room.

'I won't stay long. Just long enough to reassure myself you're all right!'

'Thank you for coming, Kim!' She said it as if she considered it proper, her pure profile turned away from him. No *real* feeling, he could see that. A strange mixture, Rory Sheridan, but her sometimes impenetrable reserve had no virtue in his eyes. He had her mother to thank for that. He was glad now he hadn't attended the funeral. Sara Sheridan's living presence seemed still to lie over the house and it would continue to do so, an essence impossible to dispel. Still, it would fetch a good price; beautiful in places, but those lofty ceilings and big open rooms couldn't be tolerated. He assessed the items of value with cynical, interested eyes. What Brendan Sheridan provided in return for abuse!

Rory would bring a nice dowry. In fact, she suited him admirably – beautiful, intelligent, unquestionably a lady, and last but not least there was the father. Sooner or later Brendan Sheridan would have to re-enter the picture. And what then? There should be endless opportunities for a prospective son-in-law. He wasn't going to be stuck in the bank all his life. But it had been solid enough for Rory's mother, almost a recommendation in itself. All in all it was impossible to reject Rory Sheridan's appeal, though he had learnt astonishingly little about her in the twelve months he had known her.

Her skin gleamed faintly opalescent under the lights. She looked very fragile, almost bewitching in the depths of the old wing-backed chair, the sheen of her robe a restless challenge. He stayed on for perhaps twenty minutes or so, making a little fitful conversation that soon lapsed. He had the disturbing impression that he wasn't quite real to her. She seemed to have retreated behind the dark veil of her lashes where his features seemed indistinct and uncertain. She went to the door with him and he held her in his arms again, murmuring that he would ring again in the morning.

Her slender, boneless body was quite still in his arms, still with a kind of utter neutrality as if her mind had gone off on an unbeaten track of its own. He made no attempt to detain her but walked quickly out into the night and moved towards the warmth and comfort of his car. He let himself in and settled in the driver's seat, looking back at her slight graceful silhouette against the glittering chandelier. Then abruptly the door closed and the light was gone.

A ripple of anger and resentment passed through him and his quick indrawn breath was stifled and harsh. It was almost as if she had shut a door in his face. Beautiful and untouchable, was she? Her skin so pale against the ruby glint of her hair. A tight frown knotted his forehead. Standing outside her tragedy, he had no patience with her grave isolation, but it was useless to try anything . . . *yet*! There was plenty of time for her to learn all the things he required in a woman.

Long, long after Kim had said good night, Rory lay awake in the darkness of her room. The house was full of sounds – the rush of the wind, the light rain against the side of the house, the creaking of old timber, the stirrings and movements in all the rooms. From downstairs she could hear the chimes of the grandfather clock. *Two o'clock!* Would it ever be daylight again? The hours of darkness were passing with deadly slowness. Just as she thought she would see in the dawn, she fell into the deep, dreamless sleep of exhaustion and awakened well after eight.

Once her eyes were open she had to get up. There was no pleasure for her now in the warmth of her bed, the patterns of sunlight that fell across the room and got caught in the filmy folds of the curtains. She had been granted a week's leave from St. Hilda's where she was Junior Art Mistress. She was bereft of all inspiration anyway. Down in the kitchen she set the percolator on the stove and made herself some toast. With a little effort she could achieve a semblance of normality.

Afterwards there were the household chores and she could lose herself for a while.

Mid-morning the post arrived. She walked down to the box and reached for the mail. A handful of sympathy cards, most of them connected with the school, and a long, grey envelope, forcefully addressed to herself, postmarked North Queensland. A sudden dryness came into her mouth and her hand trembled. She tore the envelope open quickly, standing in the cloudless winter sunlight, doubly beautiful after the grey day before. Her heart was hammering almost painfully against her rib cage.

It was quite simply a terse note and an accompanying cheque – a sizeable one. The same black scrawl of a signature on both. BRENDAN SHERIDAN.

. . . 'Now you are alone I wish you to make your home with me and my family. What is past is forgotten and better so. My solicitors will deal with the sale of the house and its contents, the proceeds of which will be made over to you. Kindly cable the date of your arrival and you will be met' . . .

Well, what did she expect? Love and kisses? She swallowed on the hard lump in her throat. There was no warmth anywhere and no sense in looking for it. Some clung to the concept of parental or romantic love as a support and a comfort, but not Rory Sheridan. She had learnt the hard way and lessons learned hard are forever remembered. This demand, in no sense a request, was obviously meant to be complied with. She knew without question that if she refused this invitation there would never be another. It was quite plainly visible between the forceful black lines.

She read and re-read the note, a stranger almost to herself. She could fling it back in his face, yet already she knew she wouldn't rest until she could pass her own judgment on the man who was her father. It was a deep-driven compulsion, swamping the loyalties her mother had commanded.

By the time Kim rang she was over the crisis, adjusting to the idea. Though it meant a parting, even if she had no intention of remaining beyond a necessary period of time, Kim was most enthusiastic about the idea, losing no time in discussing it over dinner. The restaurant was small, intimate, out of town, with an excellent cuisine. Rory only toyed with her food as she studied Kim's blond, good-looking face in the rose glow of the flower-decked lamp. His reception of her news was somewhat different from what she might have wanted.

'So you really think I should go? It would mean a separation.'

He looked up, swallowing on a tasty morsel. 'My darling girl, you'd be crazy if you didn't!' He fixed her with an amused, half impatient glance. 'We won't be apart too long if I can help it. Look at it this way. A man who sends you presents year in and year out can't be too unconcerned about you. Those pearls alone would set me back a year's salary. Your father is a big man – that's what you don't seem to appreciate. I'd be jumping for joy myself. I've made a few discreet inquiries and from all accounts he's well past his first lovely million!'

A kind of revulsion tensed her face. 'Oh, Kim, that's not my interest!'

'Well, it damned well ought to be. Rory!' Exasperation sounded in his voice. 'How naïve can you get? Listen here, sweet, there's no reason on earth why you shouldn't be your father's heir, or if we must split hairs, his heiress!'

She considered him long and thoughtfully with a dispassion that positively irritated him. 'My father has his own family, Kim. I couldn't really care if he owned the whole of North Queensland!'

'Well, he's making a fair-sized stab at it!' He leaned back and lit a cigarette without looking at her. Used to a life of restrained luxury, she had no real idea of what a grind it all was. But he *had*! If there was any short cut to *la dolce vita* he was going to take it. He looked back at her, narrowing his eyes against a veil of smoke. Her head was drooped slightly so that he was left staring at the dark slant of her brows, the heavy sweep of her lashes, the fastidious straight nose. There was no happiness in the shadowed planes of her face, only an inner intensity. The dark auburn hair, almost the ruby tint of the wine, was swept back from her face, caught in its usual, elegant knot at the nape. It suited the patrician cast of her features, but he much preferred the wild rose look he had surprised last night. Ah well, plenty of time to change that. She was speaking in a low, controlled voice, almost as much to herself as to him:

'I want to know why my father deserted me. Why my mother was forced into fleeing from him as if he were the devil himself, for God knows what detestable reasons!'

He laughed, not loudly but with open, contemptuous amusement.

'Oh, come off it, darling. Your mother was a case, a bad one. God forgive me for mentioning it at this time, but you know it was true. The driving force behind Sheridan Enterprises couldn't possibly jell with your mother's quite extraordinary estimate. All that wanton irresponsibility she was so fond of remarking upon seems rather piquant in the light of the facts!' He paused for a moment and his blue eyes glinted a challenge. 'You couldn't really say either of you lacked anything, even if your mother kept you virtually a prisoner before we met.'

She brushed pale, slender fingers over her eyes. 'You've played your hand, Kim. You won't defeat me by saying any more. Mother was difficult. I know that. Nothing can be gained by adding to that.'

He was treading delicately now on ground he knew to be dangerous. His voice was gentle, full of self-reproach.

'I'm sorry, darling, but you disturb me – or rather, your attitude disturbs me. You've been offered a great opportunity and I want you to make the most of it. You must take after your father. Do you realize that? You haven't your mother's dark eyes and dark hair. That gorgeous colouring came from somewhere – your father, most probably. In any case, there's no harm in going up and sizing up the situation for yourself. Who knows, your father might find an opening for me. I've always fancied myself a business tycoon and life in the tropics sounds rather exotic, only a step away from the Reef.' He went to refill her wine glass, but she refused, leaning her elbows on the table and staring across at him.

'You'd leave your own job?'

His mouth turned down deprecatingly. 'Of course. Just like that! I'm not all sorts of a fool, you know. A chance in a big going concern like Sheridan's has a lot more appeal than a staid old bank, though it's served its purpose.'

Suddenly she found his enthusiasm embarrassing. She drew a ragged little breath. 'You're going too far ahead, Kim!' Her voice struck a warning note, though she was really trying to imagine what it would be like to have Kim's breezy outlook. 'I have no set plan other than to get to know my father, if only slightly. He may like me. I may not like him, but I won't rest until I find out!'

22

His eyes dwelt on the creamy skin of her face and throat. It looked flawless against the sombre, dark line of her high-necked dress. Her attitude was vaguely infuriating, but he kept his voice gently concerned.

'Just don't let Sara deprive you of your birthright, that's all I ask. You are your father's only child. You might as well forget about stepchildren. They're not at all the same. Once your father sees you he can't help but want to keep you by his side, make up for all the old wrongs. Go up and have a look around. You've got nothing to lose and, who knows, a great deal to win!'

Some little light flamed and receded in the depths of her eyes. 'Has it struck you, Kim, that if I make this trip nothing might ever be the same again?'

Humour lightened his voice and sparkled from his light blue eye. 'That's something on which I'm pinning my hopes. You've got a lot to learn, darling. No man is ever one piece. Your father must have *some* sterling qualities. Find out in your own way. Just remember I want a letter every other day. Now I'm going to insist that you have something else. You've barely touched your meal. One thing is for certain, I'll never relinquish *my* claim on you!'

Reluctantly, at Kim's urging, Rory settled for a liqueur with her coffee, wishing with all her heart that she possessed even a little of his bursting good spirits. A thin stratum of her mind recognized and shied away from his calculating streak. He turned his attention from the waiter to smile into her wide, glowing eyes. There was, threaded into that warmly admiring glance, an element she didn't care to analyse. In a second it was gone and he was Kim again, the young man her mother had so much admired.

CHAPTER TWO

THE trip to the north of the continent was outside everyday experience, preceded by a week of packing and preparation, the hundred and one things that warranted her absorption; the little involuntary shivers of excitement she couldn't suppress to the sickening twist of pain and nostalgia as she looked back at the house for the last time through the rear window of a taxi bearing her away to the airport. A few special items of value or sentiment had gone into storage; the rest, house and effects, would go under the auctioneer's hammer within the next few months. It was over, all over, consigned to the limbo of the past. It made no sense at all that the old life had a hold on her so light as to be worthless. Though she allowed herself no false hopes, she still harboured the illusion, perhaps, that now at last she might find the mercy of what she had always craved, a climate of love and contentment. Only time would tell.

By the time she got to the airport the first faint butterflies of excitement were stirring. She hadn't flown very often, for her mother had disliked travel, strange people and places, living outside the comfort and privacy of her own home, so everything was touched with a special kind of novelty from the moment when she sat upright, hands loosely clasped in her lap as the jet airliner taxied down the runway, then turned to the north, gathering itself like some great silver-winged bird to soar up where it belonged, while the sprawling city fell far, far away below.

Rory unloosened her seat-belt and swallowed on the momentarily unpleasant sensation in her ears, then adjusted the seat to a semi-reclining position, tilting her head back, seeing outside the window scudding white clouds and the dense, heavenly blue of the upper atmosphere.

'Is this your first trip?' her seatmate asked in a strongly accented voice.

Rory turned her head, seeing properly for the first time a plump, handsome woman in her late forties with an Italianate complexion, long straight nose, thick, sleek black hair and the predictable fine dark eyes. There was a good-humoured tolerance in the depths of those eyes that Rory responded to.

'To the North at any rate!' she smiled. 'Does it show?'

'Only a little, young lady!' The woman spoke with lazy affability. 'You're going to the Reef like the others?'

Rory shook her head. 'I suppose at least half the passenger list are bound for Hayman or Lindeman or any one of the beautiful island retreats, but actually *I'm* not. I'm joining my father.' She tossed it off lightly as if it were the most natural thing in the world, knowing a queer little thrust of pleasure that carried her back to her schooldays when the other girls talked of their fathers and she had listened silently, her heart filled with longing.

'So!' The *signora* inclined her glossy dark head, unfailingly agreeable as lazy as a cat, wishing to follow up this piece of information, but Rory adroitly changed the subject.

'You seem a seasoned traveller yourself, *signora*?'

The woman smiled and nodded, laughing huskily in her throat, not displeased. She began to talk about her travels to the accompaniment of Latin shrugs and gestures, in the process revealing a great deal about herself and her family. She was a first generation Australian, very proud of it, but at least once in every other year she managed a trip 'home' to Italy to visit her many relations in Brezzia. Her husband and sons were in sugar and like most immigrants to the North they had done well in it. Rory was aware that about eighty per cent of the population of the far northern sugar towns were Italian or of Italian descent with a sprinkling of Spanish and Finnish thrown in. The big contribution the Italian community had made to the North and the sugar industry had been recognized in the State's centenary celebrations she remembered quite clearly from her early schooldays. She commented on this to her companion and earned for herself a beaming smile.

'You must not on any account miss the splendid sculpture by our famous artist Renato Beretta sent out from Carrara and erected on the town banks of our river – the South Johnstone, you know. It is very impressive: the Canecutter, a heroic figure, you understand, bare-chested, bearing a cane knife and a few stalks of sugar cane with an inscription in Italian, of course beginning *Ai Pionieri Dell'Industrie Dello Zucchero!*' The liquid vowels rolled off the *signora*'s tongue, giving her speech a grace her second language lacked. 'On two sides of the pediments,' she continued, 'are bas-reliefs of cane-cutters lifting heavy loads of cane on to their shoulders, resting wearily against a background of horse and plough. I feel like crying every time I see it! *Ubi bene ibi patria!* ... where the good land is, here is your country!'

'That's very beautiful, *signora!*' Rory smiled and diplomatically refrained from mentioning the fact that if the Italians were among the early pioneers of the sugar industry, they were by no means the first, as the Gaelic Innis Fail clearly proclaimed. Her own grandfather had been an Irish adventurer who settled in the North, bequeathing to his son his own love of the tropics and the islands of jade, the great twelve-hundred-mile coral rampart that beckoned across cobalt blue channels; the same Reef that had for centuries warded off those who might have reached the unknown continent, still with some parts of it uncharted, approached with great caution by oceangoing ships. She was only half listening now to the *signora*'s pleasantly informative ramblings, her mind vaulting ahead to the meeting with her father.

Once or twice she considered feigning a nap, but the half descent of her long dark lashes didn't inhibit her volatile companion in the least. The *signora* continued to effervesce about life in the tropics which obviously agreed with her, about Primo, her husband, their relatives, the multiple beauties of the North, the eternal green miles of the canefields, the massive harvesting machines, steel-jawed dinosaurs that had all but dispensed with manual labour, leaving more leisure time for the menfolk, freed now of the backbreaking task of cutting the cane under a scorching, imperious sun. Rory found she had little to do beyond insert a word here and there by way of encouragement, a state of affairs that lasted them throughout the trip.

From the moment the plane touched down she knew everything was different. There was a special warmth and brilliance in the perfume-laden air, the exciting smell of a lush, sun-soaked land, the succession of jade islands that lay gem-like across the shimmering Grand Canal, the magnificent peaks of Bellender Kerr and Bartle Frere rearing thousands of feet into the air, an indigo backdrop for the brilliant canefields that stretched back to the ranges. It was vivid, beautiful country with an expansive, easy-going character.

27

Rory said good-bye to her companion and preceded her out, murmuring a few words of thanks to the stewardess, then she walked down the stairs and on to the tarmac, feeling the caress of the tropical sun on her head and her face. She recognized her father immediately her eyes fell on him. There was no hesitation, no moment of doubt. The gay chattering crowd of tourists melted away and they were alone in the whole wide world that had gone still and quiet. He walked towards her, no more questioning her identity than she had his, his face tense to the point of grimness: a handsome, big man cleaving his way through the hemming crowd; a silver leonine head, his skin startlingly tanned, his eyes scarcely less green than her own. His gaze seemed riveted on her as if he sought to indelibly imprint her face upon his mind, his instinctive recognition paralleling her own. He reached her side, his voice matching the severity of his face, searching her face long and hard.

'A little late, Rory child, though I've kept all your duty-bound letters!'

'Father!' She was standing a foot from him, her wide, glowing eyes fixed on his face, for the moment unable to equate her two images of him, the imagining and the reality. She was infinitely relieved when a faint smile broke through the severity, the miasma that surrounded a complex, multifaceted man. Powerful hands came out to grasp her shoulders as though he had risked and won an important gamble.

'I'm not judging you, child. Nor you *me*. You're here and I'm content!'

'Thank you, Father!' she said quietly, still staring up into his face.

'Is that how you think of me?'

'I always have done!'

'Well then, Sara didn't take you entirely from me, did

28

she?' he asked harshly.

His eyes turned hard and glinting as at some personal thought. Her mother's name sounded curious on his lips, she thought, half caressing, half contemptuous. Then the bleak look faded. He looked down at her, young and very slender, tautened like a bowstring, existing only for this moment of meeting. Her grave, searching eyes were wide, glowing like a child's in their brilliance and intensity, very hard to evade.

'I don't know what to say, Rory girl! The way you look is a great pleasure to me, like rediscovering a treasure. You have a strong look of your grandmother Sheridan. I've only one worthwhile photograph of her, but you'll see what I mean.' He screwed up his eyes against the shimmering sunlight. 'I know you and I will be friends. It's in the nature of things that we should be, and I have a great deal to make up to you for.' He was frowning slightly as he spoke, but the expression in his eyes was reassuring. 'Now come along. I'll get your baggage cleared and we'll go out to the car.' He took her elbow and steered her to the terminal building. 'You can tell me all about yourself.' His voice, deep and resonant, suddenly turned faintly cynical. 'I suppose you're thinking of getting married like all the rest of your sex?'

'Not yet, Father!' she murmured almost beneath her breath.

'Engaged?'

'No!' She seemed content to go wherever he directed.

A few people turned their heads, some openly speculating as to her identity, for her father's was well known in the North, but he seemed impervious to all the curious glances, well used to them.

'There is *someone*,' he persisted. 'I can hear it in that beautifully polished voice of yours.'

'Yes, there is,' she agreed quietly. 'You're very perceptive, Father!'

'Don't I have to be!' His mouth was touched with wry amusement. 'I shall have to meet this paragon of yours, Rory. You're very young, there's plenty of time to tie yourself up for life. I'd rather see you an old maid a thousand times over than make an irretrievable and tragic mistake – my definition, at least, for an unhappy marriage. You're never free of the results of it.'

She touched his hand briefly, a curiously comforting contact. 'I'm in no hurry, Father. I want to be very sure, though Kim is as anxious to meet you as you are to meet him.'

Her father stopped in his tracks; a big man staring down at her very keenly, a hard and probing light in his eyes, not so much directed at her as through her.

'Does he now? That's interesting! Quite a lot of people want to meet me for one reason or another!' He sighed and his glance seemed to refocus. 'You don't look like a girl in love to me, Rory. There's no sparkle in your eyes, no lilt in your voice as you speak of the beloved!'

She raised her glistening head at the satirical note in his voice and he smiled. 'Personally I think it's very much a waste of time, but it does make a woman beautiful!'

'And I'm not?' The merest glimmer of mischief touched the tender curves of her mouth.

For answer her father walked on, speaking with bland calm. 'You're beautiful in the special way a young girl *is* beautiful, with promise of what is to come. You've good Sheridan bones, child. Be grateful for them. They'll last you a long time.' He turned his silver glinting head to glance at her profile. 'You're like me, Rory, I fear. When love comes it will be like a lightning strike, and God help you. You'll be lit up then, with a fine blaze under the skin. See how beautiful you'll be then. Things will be different for you – that's why I want to be around. To make sure of just that. There's been enough chaos in the Sheridan family.' He went on cloaking his real thoughts in wry humour. 'So long as you're not engaged or anything, there's no real harm done!'

She smiled but said nothing as she walked into the cool of the terminal building. Her father passed her baggage checks to a porter who quickly came up to them. The bags were located and loaded on to a trolley with miraculous speed, then wheeled at a respectful distance out to a big white Mercedes Benz parked in the shade of the pink and cerise-blossoming bauhinias.

Her father unlocked the car and Rory slipped into the bucket seat, young enough to enjoy the expensive smell of the pigskin upholstery, its comfort and luxury. She wound down the window. The sun was shining with crisp, tropic brilliance, moving north from Capricorn into Cancer. The rains were over and the winter sky a cloudless peacock blue, worth a fortune to the tourist trade as the wealthy moved from the bleak Southern States to enjoy the halcyon winter climate Queensland had to offer.

A generous tip passed hands at the rear of the vehicle, then her father was beside her, slipping behind the steering wheel, strong square hands on the wheel. She felt uncommonly elated as she realized for the first time that hitherto she had moved through life to a beat not her own. Cynical and disillusioned her father might be, but nature had provided them with an inbuilt affinity. She was as receptive to his mind as he was to hers, a fact that was instantly and mutually recognized, stilling the quivering undercurrent of old griefs and recent griefs, the rights and wrongs of things that couldn't entirely be surmounted.

31

Her father turned to smile at her. All that was formidable and autocratic had left his face. 'You don't ask
questions, do you, Rory? Very cool and composed,
quietly self-protective and very, very cautious.' Con-
trition and a kind of self-contempt throbbed in his
voice. 'Long years of training, I suppose. Between the
two of us, Sara and I have hurt you, stamped on a child's
natural exuberance!'

Her vision was suddenly blurred, but with a visible
effort she gathered the full measure of her control and
turned to smile into eyes that had momentarily betrayed
an inner desolation, an ache of bitter disappointments
and self-recriminations.

'I'm here now, Father, and that's all that matters. I
only hope I'll be of some comfort to you. You and I have
a lot to catch up on.'

He stretched out his hand and touched her cheek. The
moment of quiet desperation passed and all trace of
stress went out of his face. In front of her eyes he was
once more on course, a vigorous and successful business
man reunited to all appearances with a beloved daughter. He leaned forward and switched on the ignition and
the powerful engine purred into life.

'I'll say this for you, Rory girl – if *I* fall short of your
imaginings, you certainly don't fall short of mine.
You're everything I've ever hoped you'd be. Now let's
get on home. The family won't be there. They're over
on the island. Leonora doesn't care for flying, so it
didn't really make sense to bring them home. I have a
little business to attend to, then I'll take you across
myself.'

Rory was silent while they reversed out of the parking
lot, the big car gliding towards the entrance gates and
out on to the highway. She sat back, letting the warm
scented air brush her cheeks.

'What island is it?' she asked, looking directly at that leonine head.

'My own!' her father informed her laconically. 'Sorella, just one of the hundreds of islands and atolls strung along the Reef. It's been my private retreat for a long time now, but I'm thinking of turning it into a luxury resort to cater to the tourist trade. The Reef is big business, as you know, and the Americans usually like throwing a little money around. Besides, the island has outlived its usefulness. I rarely get time to relax and the family won't spend much time on it. They like plenty of social life, lots of travel. Everything my money can provide!'

Rory bypassed this sardonic admission, seeking only the pleasant. 'It's beautiful, I suppose, Sorella?'

'As exquisite a spot as you'll find on earth, but life has become too complicated. A man works like a dog and for what? Suddenly there comes a day when nothing seems to make much sense, all effort purposeless. Sometimes I long for the old days roaming the South Seas. A close communion with Nature is still the quickest, shortest way to contentment, peace and relaxation. A man is only rich, Rory girl, when he has a little *time* to spend, not money. Some days I think I'll hand the business over to Cal and be done with it. In a few short years I'll be sixty anyway. Up, up and away, as they say. Over the hill!'

Sunlight streamed over his deeply tanned skin, the thick silver shock of hair that had once been a few shades lighter than her own. 'You look far from over the hill, Father!' Rory said warmly, impulsively. 'You're a very handsome man!'

He considered her with evident amusement. 'Why, thank you, child. More so because you sound so delightfully sincere.'

'But I *am*! Who's Cal?' she asked lightheartedly. 'My

33

new stepbrother?'

He laughed outright. 'Good God, no! Far from it. My stepson has a bandit's approach to money. How to go through it in the shortest possible time. No, honey, Cal is my partner, my right hand. Rian McCallum. You'll be meeting him soon enough, though he may rile you a little. He has a very challenging manner with women which doesn't stop most of them from making fools of themselves over him. But he's very canny, our Cal, a real throwback to his Highland ancestors.'

Curiosity dawned in her very green eyes. 'He's not married, then, this Highland chieftain?'

'And not likely to be until he pinpoints the exact woman.' His amused glance flickered over her. 'Highland chieftain, eh? I'm damned if that's not a good description of him, and you've never even seen him!' There was a moment's pause while they swung off the highway heading towards the indigo ranges and the mile upon mile of luminous green canefields, then her father took up the threads of the conversation. 'Yes, Cal's quite a man. Steel-calibred, even if he does get my goat sometimes. In fact I think he does it on purpose just to get a little action of some kind. He has so much drive and ambition I have to keep a brake on him some part of it, otherwise we'd either end up ten times the richer or pour some good old-fashioned money down the drain and disappoint our shareholders. I'm not sure which, but Cal is sure all the time – but then he's a whole lot younger and that counts for a lot!' He broke off laughing, his eyes bright with the memory of old clashes he secretly enjoyed. He glanced at Rory's young, interested profile. 'No, Rory girl, you could never mix Cal up with anyone else!'

'He sounds very sure of himself!' she observed lightly, feeling a quite inexplicable flicker of hostility towards a cocksure, conceited, attractive-to-women Highland chieftain.

'He's that!' her father agreed amiably. 'He's got plenty of vision, Cal. It won't hurt him, at this stage, to have a little restraint on him!'

But Rory had heard enough of the intriguing Rian McCallum. Deftly she changed the subject. 'Tell me about the family.'

Unexpectedly her father's mouth went wry. 'There's not much to tell, honey. My second marriage was no more made in heaven than my first.'

'Oh, Father!'

The pathos in her clear, musical voice made him smile. Brendan Sheridan had long adjusted to realities. He turned his head briefly to smile at her. 'Don't sound so cut up about it. It's not bothering me unduly. Leonora, my wife, is happy. She has security and status. That was her goal and now she's got it. She plays her part. I've no complaints. Marc and Tonia are a little older than you are – volatile, good-looking young puppies as long as you keep up the good things of life to them. Not a thought in their glossy dark heads but pleasure. Still, you can't blame them. They were brought up that way. Everything Leonora missed out on she made sure her kids got. No, Rory child, the only woman I've ever loved was your mother, believe it or not, and even that was a disaster. At least Leonora admirably fits the role of hostess to a successful business man. She's handsome and gifted and a deft conversationalist.

'I'm not unhappy, child. I wouldn't know how to define happiness anyway. The ingredients are too complex, too elusive. Let's say, in some ways, I've missed the boat and I know it, but that's only between the two of us. You're my own flesh and blood and I know I can

35

trust you. I discuss my private life with no one. Cal guesses all my secrets, I know, but he doesn't refer to them at any rate.

'Cal is the sort of son I should and *could* have had if only your mother had given me a little time to find myself. I thought it little enough to ask, but we're all so very different. She hated my way of life and I still, to this day, can't fathom why. Still, I have my daughter now, and that means a great deal to me. Everybody has to have at least one person to turn to. All the good things of life don't mean much unless you can share them with someone you love. Then, I suppose, you might find an important ingredient of that happiness we were talking about.'

Through the open window of the car came the song of birds calling; the flash of jewelled parrot wings, a tide of movement. The bitumen hissed under the tyres. They were driving down an avenue of feathery poincianas, densely green interlocking arches that would turn to a crimson glory with the coming of the Wet, for the monsoonal rains set the wild bush to flower, the warm soil seething with life. It was then that the exquisitely decorative poincianas broke out in scarlet blossom; the cascara trees laced their hanging bean pods with yellow blooms, the brilliant, ever-present bougainvillea, violet and white and crimson, climbed in profusion, a flowering wilderness wherever one looked, and the beautiful tulip trees unfurled their burnt orange blooms.

Brendan Sheridan kept the car moving fast, pointing out this and that item of interest, stretching a hand over a landscape so green and lush that it cried out to be lain down on canvas. Rory followed his gesturing hand with her eyes, the deepening colour reflecting her eagerness and attention. Somehow they had cut through the barrier of the years, achieving the ease of long and close companionship. It was difficult to explain, but it was there all the same, that extraordinary degree of intimacy. Rory knew from the expression on her father's face that he too felt the pull of it. There would be no transition period for either of them, no feeling their way into their respective roles, for already they fitted like a second skin.

It was in a contented silence that she contemplated the emerald green canefields, full-grown cane standing ten or twelve feet high ready for harvesting in the long, idyllic months before the next monsoon. Contrasting red ochre patterns of fields lying fallow made up a brilliant mosaic under the limitless blue skies. The very perfection of the climate made the quality of light intense. She really had need of her sunglasses.

'Not far off now!' her father broke into her thoughts, as he turned the car off the bitumen and headed for a private road flanked by long lines of the graceful, flowering bauhinias. He turned his head and the message in his eyes was one she wanted to read.

'Welcome to Belguardo, my child!' The tone of his voice was deep and tender and she no longer thought of the long years of denial. All that mattered now was that the days of desertion were over. 'This was my father's life, Rory – *your* grandfather. He toiled for years to make a go of this kind of country – sugar country. Only a decade ago it was the toughest, most back-breaking work there was for a white man. In the bad old days of blackbirding men from the Gilberts and Spice Islands were shanghaied for work in the canefields. You can still see the results of it along the coast – curious racial mixtures, Orient and Island inter-marriages. In my father's day it was thought there would never be mechanical ways of harvesting cane. Now, of course, it's happened. Australia leads the world in the mechanical cultivation and harvesting of the crop. If you remember Ray Lawler's play, "Summer of the Seventeenth Doll" you'll find it's far out of date. Men no longer break their backs and their health on the canefields. My father did just that. It was a great satisfaction to me to be able to buy back this exact piece of land and add to it – better still, to make it *pay*. In my father's day, seventy thousand tons was considered a good seasonal figure for this district. Now we crush the same load in a week with five times the yield on exactly the same ground. You'll be able to watch the whole operation from A to Z. Know anything about sugar?'

'Not much more than that I take a teaspoonful in my coffee!'

'No sweet tooth?' he smiled.

'Only for chocolate!'

'I'll remember that. But you'll know a whole lot more about sugar in a very short time, though it's only a quarter of my interests. I dabble in a lot of things. Our giant grass *saecharum* originated in the New Guinea Zone. They started to grow cane commercially just outside of Brisbane in the 1860s. You really should know that Captain the Hon. Louis Hope is called the "Father" of the industry. Anyway, the soil in Brisbane wasn't very suitable and they shifted the industry to the North. Needless to say, cane became the eternal presence up here. It thrives like nowhere else, the only crop men live by in these parts. This lot is about ripe for harvest. I'll wait until Cal gets back from the Gulf, then we'll fire the crop by night. It's a sight you're never likely to forget. You can watch the harvesters cutting the cane. Cranes load it on to the diesel for transport to the mills. When we're on in the season I'll take you over our biggest refinery. If I say so myself, the flow of production is pretty impressive – trainload after trainload

38

of freshly cut cane coming in from the fields. Endless lines of conveyor belts drawing it into the crushers, the ceaseless hum of the giant retorts, the huge, circular dryers processing the brown crystallized sugar and always and everywhere the heavy, sweet smell of molasses.'

He turned to her, his face animated, happy and relaxed. 'Then when you get tired of sugar either Cal or myself will take you along with us when we visit our properties in the Gulf Country. Cattle. Big business out there, and there's always the Reef, my first and my last love, one of the great natural wonders of the world. So beautiful, so frightening, so intricately fashioned, so much a legend and a challenge to any sailor. I'll never grow tired of it and I couldn't live far from it. Have you ever been to one of the usual resorts?'

Rory nibbled a little defensively on her lip. 'Actually Mother. . . .'

'. . . I know!' her father cut in on her. 'Sara never did like travel or outside influences. She was like a tabby cat on the home hearth, rarely straying far from it. But you're like me. There's a whole wide world waiting for you, so much I can show you. But your own country first. If I haven't the time, and God knows I've precious little of it, I'll make Cal show you around.'

'*Make* him?' Even with Rory's scant knowledge of the man called McCallum she found the word incongruous. So apparently, on reflection, did her father. He laughed aloud.

'A decided slip. No one can make Cal do anything. Let's say he has a fine eye for beauty in any form, and you *are* beautiful, my litle girl.'

'Not so little,' Rory smiled, her eyes green and glittery with excitement. 'I'm a bit above average height.'

39

'And why wouldn't you be?' her father protested. 'I'm over six feet myself and Cal certainly doesn't look up to anyone either!'

'You like him very much, don't you, Father? This McCallum. I can hear it in your voice.'

Her father smiled across at her with some special shade of meaning. 'Um! *I* like him, though I'm warning you there's no inbetween state where Rian is concerned. He's that kind of man. Now look straight ahead. The house is coming up. I like it from this angle best of all. I only wish the old man could have seen it. He would no more have believed it than your mother, God rest her soul. I could never forget in a lifetime the day she hurtled you both out of my life, though it was only a note she left me. Ah well, Bren Sheridan has made good. That charming rogue!' His voice altered suddenly. 'It will be yours, Rory, when I'm gone. Yours and your children's.'

'Mine, Father?' She couldn't keep the amazed incredulity out of her voice.

He nodded his head forcefully. 'Would I be leaving it to anyone else? You're my own flesh and blood. There's no substitute for that. You're a Sheridan. You'll love the land, cherish it. You're your grandmother all over again with all her fire and vitality banked down. But you'll come to life again, Rory, my girl, in the heat and exotica of the tropics, or I'll be wanting to know why. You've lived long enough under restraint. Restraint of the spirit, perhaps. I can see it. It shows. But it won't be necessary from now on. My daughter is free to do as she wishes, answerable to no one, not even me. Now tell me what you think of your inheritance?'

He turned on her like a judge awaiting the verdict, his face almost stern.

'Please let me get my breath back!' There was

40

mingled shock and rapt pleasure in her face. 'Is this a secret between us?'

He lifted one hand off the wheel to slice the air emphatically. 'Good God, no! It's always been my intention to leave you Belguardo even if you'd refused my invitation. I'll admit now, the night I composed it I was in a pretty bleak mood and none too sober. Your mother's death affected me too, Rory, though I don't really expect you to believe it. One can't cut off feeling for a person because they find you and your way of life unbearable. Once a long time ago your mother cut deep to the heart of me and I've never forgotten it. One carries the old raptures long after the misdeeds have faded. If Sara and I had used our heads instead of our hearts we would never have married in the first place, but then where would you be? You see, Rory, good can come out of the most bitter experiences. I'd like to think so anyway. See what you've done for me already? I'm no longer the complete cynic. My daughter has been returned to me!'

'Stop the car, Father. I'd like to get out. Here, just on the crest of the rise.'

He obeyed her voice, its subtle, moving quality. She had picked her own vantage point and it matched his own. The big car came to rest on the grassy verge and they stepped out, coming together, her father's arm on her shoulder as they looked up at Belguardo, set like a swan on a green lake of grass. It was big, snow white and immaculate in the classical tradition. Clear-cut and symmetrical; a colonnaded two-storied central section, flanked on either side by one-storey wings, its lines flowing upwards and outwards into the perfect whole. A deep noonday quiet pervaded the atmosphere sleeping under the hot sun. Nothing within sight seemed to stir or to move.

The trees threw a golden green haze over their faces. Rory gazed for a long time, then she looked up, meeting the proud little smile on her father's face.

'I never expected anything so beautiful,' she said with grave courtesy. 'It's like a swan gliding over a rippling sea of green!'

All Brendan Sheridan's long-held defences seemed to crumble before the expression on his daughter's face. She had a look of belonging, a natural right to be standing there on the rich red soil looking out over Belguardo, her inheritance. The soft, warm air, the exotic setting seemed to agree with her. Her small head with its delicately determined chin was thrown up, the sun caught in the rich dark red of her loosely coiled hair. The hand on her shoulder trembled slightly and he turned his profile sharply, feigning a matter-of-fact tone.

'I gave the architect a free rein with only one stipulation – none of the unconventional new-fangled designs for me. I like the elegant, the old and the gracious. All these *tomorrow* designs leave me cold. They lack character, commonplace for all the money spent on them. I didn't want a luxury motel with a set place for every stick of furniture, I wanted a home combining the best of the past with all the present can offer. I think our man attained a degree of perfection, don't you? Clever sort of fellow, not long out from the Old Country, so he had a fair idea of what I wanted. I've some beautiful pieces I've collected over the years. You can feast your eyes on them to your heart's content, for they'll all be yours and no one else going short, so don't be bothered about *that*!' His voice wavered slightly, but he kept his eyes trained on the house. 'Well, Rory my girl, what do you say?'

There was suddenly tears in her glowing, green eyes, misting her vision, but she didn't blink them away. 'I think I've come home, Father!' she said with perfect simplicity, and rested against his strong, yielding shoulder. Warmth flooded through her for which she had no resistance, for the thaw in her blood had already begun. This was Belguardo. Here was her father. The wheel of fate had spun full circle and come to rest.

CHAPTER THREE

THE next few days passed in a fine blaze of happy re-
union. A short enough space of time, yet time that had
quality to it, with the capacity to remain fresh and
endless in the memory long after other days were forgotten: emotional at times when all the old awkward
hurts were approached, but for the most part touched
with a warm sense of rightness, a completeness that left
Rory shedding a few tears into her pillow at night. Not
the slow, sad tears of old hurts and frustrations, but the
quick easy tears of heightened emotion, a heart long
denied, brimming now with a new-found richness and
content.

There was some special magic about that time on
Belguardo that would never be lost to her; the redis-
covery of a father who loved her, the house, its beauty,
the red earth, the green canefields, the crisp vital air, a
dancing mirage to enchant and baffle the sight. There
was so much to see, so much to be learnt, but for the
present she and her father had large areas of their separate lives to cover. It was no longer a small miracle, but
an established fact between them, their deep sense of
rapport, the inherent bond of understanding, streng-
thened by so many shared characteristics; a gentle
gaiety, a wry sense of humour, and underneath that sur-
face self-containment, warm, generous emotions.

At the end of the week they were to leave for the
island Sorella, an uplifted coral island with tall coconut
palms and pandanus clustered at its edge, floating on a
sea 'so brilliantly blue as to defy description', her father
had said. The island itself could offer nothing but en-

44

chantment. It was the human involvements that caused Rory some slight trepidation. If her father's family accepted her, all would be well, but it was by no means certain that they would. She wasn't a child to be threaded into the overall pattern, but a complete adult with set and unchanging characteristics. She could only hope and wait. If fate continued to smile on her they would like and accept her.

Dutifully she had sent off a letter to Kim and puzzled afterwards that that was what the writing of it had amounted to ... a duty! Perhaps it was because so much that was new and exciting was happening to her. With this thought she consoled and excused herself. How could she forget the warmth and the friendliness Kim had brought into her life? As soon as it could be conveniently arranged he would be here on Belguardo. It would surpass even Kim's expectations, she thought a little wryly, conscious of his hankerings after the good things of life, or the so-called 'good things' all that wealth and position could offer.

Dinner would be late that night. Her father had spent most of the afternoon out on business, only to arrive home with a huge box under his arm and the air of a man who had achieved a sensational bargain. It proved to be an item of feminine apparel that had caught his eye and convinced him it would suit his daughter's colouring to perfection. It did. Much later in her room Rory tried it on and decided she would wear it down to dinner. It would give her father pleasure, at least as much as it did her. She stood in front of the long mirror twirling idly, studying her reflection. It was beautiful – a hostess gown, rather romantic, in pumpkin-coloured velvet, with a slight medieval look, perhaps the gold thread criss-crossing the long tight sleeves and outlining the low oval neckline, the skirt falling in supple folds to

45

her feet.

She debated brushing her hair out but finally looped it at the nape with a beaten gold clasp, feeling, mistakenly, that this was essentially her style. Already she could feel a difference in herself, see a difference in her appearance. Her eyes were no longer shadowed but startlingly clear, fringed by a dark density of lashes in contrast to her deep auburn hair. It was a beautiful night, a little crisp after the golden warmth of the day. She padded about her room a little aimlessly, perfectly content, then stepped into her shoes. It must be getting on towards seven.

She glanced about her room again with the now familiar rush of pleasure, absorbing its delicate, feminine ambiance. Her father had shifted a collection of opaline glass into it for her never-ending private enjoyment. It shone, richly blue, from a lacquered Regency cabinet. Heavy gold-framed Italian flower prints glowed from the pale, pale walls; an original watercolour over the huge bed with its beautiful spread, a delicate tracery of wild flowers, some echoing the Bristol blue of the glass collection. A day bed, upholstered in the same fabric, was placed against the window wall to look out over the garden; a writing desk and chair in front of a small antique armoire containing books and fine china objects, flanked by two wing-backed deeply upholstered armchairs. Her father had told her she could redecorate it as she pleased, but she had no inclination to change a thing, not realizing that, perversely feminine, she had in fact rearranged the chairs.

She lingered a while longer, fastidiously tidying the dressing-table, then she flicked off the light and went out into the passageway. The house seemed very quiet. There was a household staff of two; a husband-and-wife team, a couple of Italian extraction, the wife an excellent

46

cook and housekeeper, the husband equally capable in tending the extensive grounds, yet there wasn't a sound from anywhere. Probably her father was still dressing. She came on down the beautiful circular stairway, admiring her own flower arrangement in the entrance hall. Quite suddenly out of the silence of the house came the sound of two voices – one her father's, a little quizzical, calmly reasonable, the other younger, firmer, unknown to her, spiked with a half amused anger, diabolically self-assured. She experienced a half-formed wish to flee from that voice, moving instinctively against the wall, the light bracket throwing a warm amber glow over the side of her face and head. Her father's voice came again, mildly interrogative:

'Are you sure you're not confusing facts with dreams? You know what Baxter has to say.'

'To hell with what Baxter has to say!'

That firm resonant voice with its fine cutting edge would always be annihilating. She listened intently as if her mind and her body had clenched themselves together.

'. . . He's nothing but a desk-bound accountant, anyway. Any dreams he had were soon dissipated. I tell you, Bren, the whole scheme is a winner. It only needs a little rethinking of all Baxter's stale theories. I've unearthed a few of these facts you're so interested in. Take a look at them!'

The library door was suddenly flung open and a man emerged – tall, lean, powerfully built. Dark, very definite features; the nose high-bridged and imperious, the mouth wide, rather sensuous, hollows under the high cheekbones, deep lines running from nose to mouth, a chin as deeply cleft as if from the indentation of a forefinger. The whole impression was one of force and a dark, leashed vitality, emphasis and excitement

47

cleaving two vertical lines between his ink-dark brows.

Shock, the first shock was moving out to her, though she had wished it all on herself. This man would never befriend her, not in a lifetime. She stood there locked in a curious tension, a kind of anxious hope dread when all along she knew the answer. The thought of it was like a blow, threatening her frail peace. The man threw up his head and saw her, her face as pale as the hand she held to her throat, the light glossing the velvet sheen of her gown, catching the glinting gold thread. His glance seemed to leap over her, his eyes the second shock; ice grey, clear and brilliant. They had the power to transfix her, so totally a surprise that immediately she threw up her own defences, the strict rules of discipline she had long imposed on herself. *Don't run away from the things that frighten you. Face up to them.* It was a case of mind over matter. This man was a threat and a challenge, and he was only a few feet away. Pride and convention demanded that she find her voice. It sounded small, rather cold, unbearably formal even to her own ears.

'I beg your pardon. Am I intruding?'

He was swiftly something else – worldly, aware, well versed in the ways of women, smiling with smooth, taunting courtesy, his dark masculinity a live thing.

'On no account. I'm enchanted and *calmed*, Miss Sheridan. McCallum at your service!'

If there was such a thing as sexual radiance, he had it. Those strange eyes went over her swiftly, comprehensively. In any account of her there would not be a detail missing. He moved a few paces towards her, standing directly under the sparkling, shadow-free light of the Waterford chandelier. It glanced off his dark face; proud, even ruthless, the face of a man in undisputed

48

possession of every horizon in sight, yet those very qualities were part of his undeniable attraction. The rest of the world was there, but somehow to Rory it seemed quite separate.

He appeared to be watching her with the uncanny concentration of a cat with a mouse. She came on down the stairs with graceful, gliding movements, her long skirt fluid about her feet. There was the sound of a chair scraping as her father eased himself out of his swivel chair and came to the library door, a deep note of pleasure in his voice.

'A good piece of timing, darling, even if no one, but no one beats Cal to the punch. May I second that introduction? Rian McCallum, my partner, failing anyone more suitable . . .!' He cast the younger man an amused, sardonic glance that met with a faint relaxation about the shapely mouth.

She stood there, clearly exposed against the brilliant backdrop of light, as she turned to face him.

'How do you do, Mr. McCallum!' She gave him her hand with scrupulous courtesy, warm colour tinting her cheekbones. The expression in his crystal clear eyes was disturbing, faintly mocking. Something appeared to be amusing the man and she hated the sensation that she was the cause of it.

He took the pale, slender fingers outstretched to him. 'Nothing like that. Rian, please!'

Her hand tingled away almost immediately, surrendering the brief contact. 'Forgive me,' she said gently, 'my memory was being overtaxed with the Cals and the Rians and the McCallums!'

'I don't wonder!' His eyes went glittery, clearly intent upon her. Her blood began racing. She could feel it rushing to her head. She thought it was anger, a deep-driven defence to meet an insolence and fiery pride the like of which she had never yet encountered.

He flickered a glance over her face and she felt it come burningly alive. 'That couldn't be hostility in those emerald green eyes? I can't say I've ever cared for green eyes in a woman, but now I've the distinct feeling I'm seeing them for the first time!'

Her father gave a soft, gusty laugh in his throat. 'Have a heart, Cal! Give the child time to get used to you. You'll stay to dinner, won't you? No trouble at all to set another place.'

'May I stay to dinner, Miss Sheridan?' He turned on her suavely, surprising her own piercingly little scrutiny.

'I'm hoping you will!'

The firm mouth relaxed a little. 'In that case I will. Life holds nothing more rewarding than the company of a beautiful woman!'

Her father was gazing from one to the other, a lively amused expression on his face. 'Never trust a Scot! Take it all with a grain of salt, Rory girl. McCallum's notorious!'

'No call for alarm, Bren. Your daughter has already taken my measure.'

'In that case I'll go change for dinner with fresh heart. Make yourself at home, Cal – not that you won't anyway. I won't keep you long.'

Bren Sheridan prepared to move off, halted by his partner's voice.

'You might ring Dowling while you're at it!'

'Will do. Rory darling, I'll leave you to look after our guest. I'll tell Maria on the way out.'

She could feel her heart beating rapidly. She looked away from that autocratic dark head walking into the library, feeling his presence behind her. Danger and intrigue were well enough for those who wanted it. She didn't. His voice, dark and vibrant as the rest of him, reached her easily.

'In a damnably odd day, you're the damnedest!'

She turned quickly on impulse, her skirt swirling, then falling in long supple folds. 'I don't follow you.'

'Why would you?' he agreed. 'A velvet madonna – aloof, serene, untouchable. A more discerning eye might see that you are, in fact, none of these things!'

She tried and succeeded in keeping the heat out of her voice. 'I've no doubt you've some experience?'

'A little!' He nodded his dark head agreeably. 'By all the laws of human compensation, your name should be Maggie or Agatha or something equally dreary. But *Rory*! It's too much!' He moved easily across the room with meticulous grace. 'Come away from those curtains. They're too good a background. Allow me to fix you a drink. No? You won't mind if I finish mine? Let's say, Rory, you're not what I expected.'

'Oh!' She looked away from those calculating grey eyes, deliberately studying the casual perfection of his jacket as a form of relief.

'The scent of jasmine – disturbing, misleading. I rather expected someone altogether different.' He tossed his drink off as if to strengthen his assertion.

'You're disappointed, of course.' She felt oddly keyed up, yet her voice was commendably cool for a young girl.

'Did I say so?' His glance was intense, a sharp silver-grey.

'It's what you're *not* saying that's getting to me, Mr. McCallum,' she said crisply. 'Perhaps it's time we stopped beating about the bush!'

He laughed suddenly, his eyes gleaming, and she wished that he hadn't, for his smile called attention to qualities she would rather overlook. Her heart began to hurt and the blood rushed through her body to her fingertips, warming her. She turned her head swiftly and he was left talking to her pale, pure profile.

'Apart from that haunting little sense of familiarity, that expression, if nothing else, seals your identity. I couldn't count the number of times I've heard Bren use it, in almost exactly the same tone of voice!'

She looked away very carefully from that tantalizing smile. 'Yet you still don't trust me. Why?'

'In short, you're *trouble*!' he murmured succinctly, his mouth cool and cynical. 'Some women go through life without creating a ripple. I'm forced to conclude, that you're not in that category!' His rapier glance noted her mute protest and he lifted his hand in a gesture that made all denials unimportant. 'Don't look at me like that! You're like the bird freed too soon from the cage. You don't quite know what to do with your freedom. Your father is a very wealthy man. Neither of us can overlook that fact. Not me, his partner. Not you, the long-lost daughter, fifteen years too late!'

'You take my breath away!' It was hard to sound cool and uncaring with an awful constriction in her breast.

'Anything else?' he asked, a flash of sarcasm in that vibrant voice that quickly turned serious, queerly judicial, detached and powerful. 'Don't hurt him, will you? I know what a woman can do to a man – the wives, daughters, lovers. Right now your father is on top of the world, a king in a world of your making. I've never seen him like that before. I'd like it to stay that way and only you can topple him off – the new-found centre of his universe!'

She shook her deeply glistening head, a bewildered frown between her winged dark brows. 'You've too much imagination!'

'A penetrating analysis!' There was a wicked flare of

devilry in his eyes, sensually alive. 'And you have all the physical qualifications! That little touch of mystery and aloofness that attracts a man in the first place – but I was inoculated early, my child, one builds up a resistance. A man has a lot to learn about women, and the first thing he learns is there are many different kinds of them. Mostly the wrong kind!'

She regretted the quick heat in her cheeks but she couldn't control it. Anger leapt like a flame. 'Of all . . . !'

'. . . the unmitigated gall!' he cut her off laconically. 'That's how it goes, doesn't it, my sweet little innocent? The trick is, how to get on with me. For you'll have to, won't you, *Rory*?'

The sound of her own name almost shocked her, delivered with such intimacy, a caressing inflection that flagrantly denied the distance she was trying to maintain between them. Curious and frightening the trick some voices had to them to portray manifold fine shadings.

His quick eyes narrowed over her. 'That's right, isn't it? Understand and tolerate all the insouciance that's making your eyes glitter. I wondered when you'd come real, but even a spun glass madonna has a limit of tolerance, it seems!'

She moistened her bottom lip and looked at him almost fearfully. 'Why glass?'

'Why not? That guise could be shattered in an instant!'

She felt oddly at sea, shivering as though she had taken a chill in the soft lambent air. 'We seem to be at war, Mr. McCallum!'

'That goes without saying. With no immediate prospect of getting rid of me. One way and the other I've gotten used to protecting your father's interests. I'm going to keep an eye on you, *bellissima*. I'm sorry, but until you've proved yourself that's the way things are!' There was a hard note of finality in his voice for all the superficial charm of his smile.

'I only hope I can! Prove myself. I mean!' she commented.

'Well ... so do I. But there are certain definite requirements!'

She stared at him, aware of the night, the warm tropical scents it released. His air of relaxation was curious, for all along she had the feeling that it could be instantly transmuted to explosive action. 'You're mad!' she managed at last as though they were the only words that occurred to her.

His grey eyes glinted, a flickering light in them. 'You said that before, or something very like it!'

Every nerve inside her was tautening in breathless succession. 'You don't appear to have a very high regard for women, Mr. McCallum, but let me tell you we can't be classified quite as easily as you'd like to make out. I don't wonder you're not married!'

Nothing, it seemed, could penetrate the façade of his easy, urbane manner. 'But then I'm like the happy Frenchman, Miss Sheridan, a bachelor at heart. Anything else calls for too much wear and tear on the nervous system!'

'I think I will have a drink!' she said faintly.

He turned to smile at her, a real smile this time, with laughter springing into his eyes, not only a twist of that ironic mouth. 'I see you have the gift for instant transition!'

'Not at all. Suddenly I feel the need of one!'

'Wise girl! Put an end to this unequal contest. You won't win. Not with me, little one!'

'Forgive me if I estimate my own chances!' She took a deep breath as she watched him turn away to a modular unit that lines one wall. A central section already lay open, to display a selection of crystal glasses in all shapes and sizes and a large assortment of spirits and sherries and liqueurs. He didn't ask her what she wanted but poured some dry vermouth over cracked ice, garnishing it with a slice of lemon, both from the tiny wall refrigerator built into a section directly above it.

He walked back towards her holding out the glass. 'Cinzano!'

'I've never tried it before.'

'We've all got to take the plunge some time! Why not drink to *our* partnership?'

'So long as there's no question of my having to like you, Mr. McCallum!' she said with a touch of his own irony.

'Not the slightest!' He mocked her over the rim of her glass. 'Just pretend that you do, for your father's sake. You're here and you'll stay for however long it suits him. *This* time!'

'Have no fear, I will. Even if it kills me!' She set her glass down quickly only half finished, losing all caution.

'Thank you. I quite see the nobility of that. No expense spared and all that. That's a singularly beautiful gown you're wearing. This might seem like a crisis to you, Rory, but in reality it's only a testing period. You're an adult now, so you'll appreciate the need for it.'

'I appreciate the fact that you bear no resemblance whatever to any man I've ever known!'

He shrugged his wide shoulders carelessly, tolerantly at her painful intensity. 'I take no offence at that, though I suppose I should. How old are you anyway? Twenty? And a young twenty at that! Guarding your glances – everything. I don't think you know a great deal about men.'

He leant away from her and reached for a cigarette. She could feel her face flaming with the knowledge of her own immaturity, all the time fighting the traitorous wish that things could be different between them. But the stage was set and they were inevitable antagonists. Realization of that would save her trouble. She heard her own voice continuing with a hint of wry humour:

'You're very unconventional, Mr. McCallum!'

'So are *you*!' He was regarding her steadily, his light eyes narrowed against the thin veil of smoke.

'I am not!' she said quickly, convinced of the truth of it.

'Yes, you are. There's no need for a morsel of shame. It was the first thing I noticed about you.' He looked very tall, cool and calculating with his back to the light.

'Well, you'll have to forgive my blank confusion now. I just feel totally inadequate, though I imagine you're well used to that kind of a reaction. This promises to be a very strange alliance indeed!'

'If that's what it *is*. Just remember to keep it natural. No contrivance about it. A devious enough dodge for a woman!'

Her voice sounded a little shaken, genuinely bewildered.

'I'm afraid not, Mr. McCallum. I find it a very tall order indeed!'

'Perhaps your mind is too conventional?' He moved so swiftly she could scarcely credit he was beside her, his eyes glittering over her tilted head. 'And why in the world do you wear your hair like that? Hair like yours is meant to swing free. All those magic little moves across the face and cheeks – no woman can afford to be without them!'

The quality of his glance was so lit by sheer devilry that she almost retreated a step. His hand came up in a sleek co-ordinated movement to flick at the clasp that caught back her hair, catching it neatly as it slipped along the heavy silken strands on its way to the carpet. She jerked her own head back distractedly, her hand going up in an involuntary gesture to smooth back the heavy forward sweep of hair, but he encircled her wrist, imposing the lightest restraint upon it.

'No, leave it!'

The blood glittered like fire in her veins. 'Mr. McCallum, I hate you! *Hate* you!' Her small poised head was thrown up, her wide eyes glowing. The light made a ruby glinting mist of her loose hair, each strand palpitating in the golden light that poured down from directly above them. Her face came alive with quick feelings, losing its creamy aloofness, flooded with colour, burningly alive.

'Well, well, well!' There was a wholly masculine look on his dark face, his voice speculative. 'Only don't put too much weight into that *hating*. I might believe you!'

'I'm sorry to disappoint you, but it's true! Or it's true right at this minute. Nothing and no one prepared me for *you*, Mr. McCallum. I find the whole situation unbelievable!'

'I'm inclined to agree!' He gave her a long, level look that turned into a flash of a smile. 'But then you're not what I expected either. Not what any of us expected. Excluding perhaps Bren, and God knows he's happy enough with what he got!'

Anger bred from a dozen different emotions reached flashpoint. 'Are you jealous, Mr. McCallum?' she flashed at him.

He appeared to consider it gravely, then laughed.

'Don't be absurd, child. Though it's a slick enough theory and done to death!'

'The basic emotions are never done to death, Mr. McCallum,' Rory said in a poignant little voice. 'I don't deal in ulterior motives myself, so you won't blame me if I don't see things your way!'

'But you do, *Rory*!' There was a challenging set to his lean, lithe body. 'You're in all too deep. One of the rewards of a girl who likes to live dangerously!'

She stared up at him with trancelike concentration, registering every detail of his dominant dark face. 'I'm sure you're brilliant at your job, but you're on the wrong track entirely *this* time!'

Cynicism touched his clearly defined mouth. 'Reassure me, then. I'm putty in the hands of the right woman. One thing is certain, you're no quitter, not with that delicately determined little chin!' His glance was half amused, half irritated. 'Winter might be ahead, but I feel we shall see the spring!'

Her breath almost caught and she turned away with fierce urgency. 'The thought doesn't thrill me, but you offer no alternative. In my own defence I might say you do me an injustice. Father had the foresight to mention that you might rile me a little, but he omitted to add that you're a very militant crusader. Quite insufferable, in fact!'

'Now that I just cannot accept!' he said in a soft, amused voice. 'Any more than I can allow you to harbour any such delusion. I've always enjoyed women's company and they mine. In fact there's not a one of them refused to speak to me on the telephone next morning!'

He turned his head to her, his light eyes dancing, quite brilliant with mockery. 'Perhaps you're a little off balance. Some slight disturbance to the equilibrium?'

Her voice was a pale ghost of itself. 'I've changed my mind. You're not insufferable at all, you're a gentleman. Anyone can see that!'

'That drink has gone to your head, *cara*. There are no gentlemen left! But if we must resurrect that forgotten race I hear you *have* a suitor! I'd be interested to meet him.'

'You will, Mr. McCallum, I can promise you that!' Her voice sounded oddly defensive and she didn't intend it that way at all.

His eyes were travelling over her face like a shock of electric current. 'Fascinating! It gets better and better. I hear he works in a bank!'

He sounded solemn and insulting at once – the faint stress on *bank* a masterpiece in insolence, as if a bank were the last place in the world an aspiring young man would wish to find himself an employee.

'I'm *trying* to like, you, Mr. McCallum,' she said to the back of his dark head, surprised to find she was trembling a little, 'but it can't be done!'

'You'll find a way, you'll see!' he said crisply watching, with interest, her agitated little movements round the room.

'. . . or die trying!' She came to a halt directly in front of him, but her hesitation was a mistake. It was better to keep moving. Anywhere away from those eyes.

'You look like a wild rose,' he said with faint amusement. 'Or close enough to the picture you're making. Another turn around the room and you'll have me quite giddy. Try to relax, child!'

It was an impossible situation and she was hopelessly out of her depth, yet she made a determined effort to smother a rising sense of exasperation. She had known of this before. It had always been there. This scene.

This man. This enemy. Total disaster with his black head thrown up, grey eyes sharpening, lightening to the colour of old heirloom silver, the line of his mouth curved in – *triumph*? If it wasn't triumph she didn't know what it was. The rich satisfaction of knowing himself master. She felt almost bemused, desperately in need of a breathing space. His eyes were on her, suavely pensive, and rather helplessly she moved back into the comparative safety of one of her father's huge black leather-upholstered chairs. It was a piquant foil for her slender femininity.

He was silent for a moment, his mouth, shapely and mobile, changing according to his mood. Now it smiled.

'Why don't you finish your drink and sit quietly? In other circumstances I might find you irresistible, watching me like an unwinking cat – green eyes glowing, cool, very faintly hostile.'

He passed her glass to her – good hands, long-fingered, strong and brown. Hands that could. . . . She shut down on the chaotic direction of her thoughts, vaguely ashamed of them. There was a dreadful sureness about the way he moved, supple, loose-limbed, standing before her studying her as if she were an antique whose authenticity was in question. Had the physical resemblance between her father and herself not been so marked she would have been decidedly suspect in that direction as well. There was simply no place in her life for Rian McCallum. The thought depressed and excited her at once, two conflicting emotions catching her up in a strong undertow, making her tense and wary. Her green eyes were as luminous as a piece of Venetian glass. She could no more make a friend or an ally of Rian McCallum than tame the great wedge-tailed eagles that soared over the canefields. She gave him a quick, oblique look, only to find him watching her, a mocking kind of indulgence on his dark face.

'Chin up! The situation only seems fraught with difficulties. This too will pass. Meantime I've accomplished enough – for the moment!'

There was the sound of footsteps in the hall and he turned his dark head over his shoulder. 'That's your father, determined to make good friends of us. For God's sake, smile!'

A reply occurred to her, but she could hardly give voice to it with him towering above her, darkly, vividly, masculine. Her father walked through the open doorway, vigour in his step, a smile on his face, the epitome of the warmly hospitable host. 'What about a drink before dinner? It's all set with Maria. It seems you're one of her favourites, Cal!'

'Sensible woman!' McCallum rejoined lazily.

Brendan Sheridan looked across at his daughter, a little disconcerted by the tangible change in her. She was sitting there wrapped in her own atmosphere, colour shining across her cheekbones, her eyes strangely secretive, the light flashing out the ruby tints of her hair.

'You look disturbed, darling.'

She smiled reassuringly. 'Nothing important!'

'Anything that disturbs you *is* important!' her father maintained. 'Rian?' he cocked his silver head to his partner.

The wide shoulders shrugged negligently. 'I'm afraid I can't be of much practical help, Bren. Rory and I were only indulging in some pleasant, inconsequential chatter. Don't you believe me?'

'Not altogether. In fact if I had a cent for every time you put me off the track I'd soon be rich!' Bren Sheridan's smile was sharp with amused derision.

'What on earth does he mean?' the silver-grey glance

61

was transferred to Rory, appealing to her. It was too much, under the circumstances. He smiled at her silence, leaning back against the desk, his voice lazy with urbane good humour. 'You have a curious sense of humour, Bren!'

'Never mind! To my credit I admit I can't do without you!'

'Don't say it as if it were of such little concern. Did you ring Dowling?'

And now he was the business man ready and able to put anyone's head on the chopping block, his voice hard-edged, serious all of a sudden. Her father laughed, affection and awareness of the younger man's nature in his voice.

'God, Cal, you remind me of those medieval chargers rearing, plunging, into the fray. Let's have dinner first. It might aid your digestion if I tell you he's backed down as usual. Now what's that you've got, darling? Cinzano?' Bren Sheridan walked away to the wall unit. 'I didn't tell you how beautiful you look. You must admire my taste, Cal. That velvet was my choice.'

'And infinitely successful!' McCallum cut in smoothly, inclining his dark head towards Rory. 'I've already complimented your daughter.' In the shadow-free light he was the embodiment of male chivalry, a benevolent overlord, only his eyes, a clear, lambent grey, were alight with pure devilment, some pulsing inner amusement.

Rory looked away carefully from that shrewd assessment, pinning her gaze to a spot between her father's broad shoulders, as her only hope. McCallum noted the manoeuvre with a devastating twist to his mouth. Bren Sheridan turned back to them, handing them a glass in turn, his eyes smiling, his voice warmly reflective.

'Life is so short, so full of heartbreak that one must hold on to these moments. To love, really love someone, a wife, a husband, your child, is the only true joy. You'll find that out one day, Rory. I've lived a long time with just the shadow of my girl, wondering what sort of a woman she'd grown into. Now, for the life of me, I can't imagine spending the rest of my days without her!'

Rory moved swiftly, impulsively, rising to her feet, coming across to her father, tipping her face to kiss his darkly tanned cheek. 'Thank you, Father!'

They made an arresting tableau, the two of them together, the big, silver-haired man, the slender young girl at his side, in her beautiful gown, but Rory was unaware of it, her whole attention trapped, for across the clear space of the room she looked directly into a pair of eyes that sparkled with the desire to outwit, out-manoeuvre, and eventually manipulate her for some purpose of his own. But what? Even in the stress of her thoughts she was convinced he could read her mind. The sweet delusion that everything would be all right was shattered. Foolishly she had been trying to live a dream for herself. Rian McCallum had jerked her back to her senses. Her only hope was to develop a hard, protective shell against him. But how?

CHAPTER FOUR

SHE was dreaming of the island. The feathery tops of coconut palms waving in the breeze, a dazzling white boomerang of beach, the sun on water that changed from ultramarine to the cool, translucent green of the enclosed lagoon and beyond the reef, the surf shooting silvery plumes into the air, beating against the coral crenellations. Birds were singing. The whole, glowing world was alive with birdsong, piercingly beautiful.

It was a waking dream, for the early morning breeze forced its coolness through the wide open windows, prickling her skin, carrying the scent of countless flowers. She opened her eyes to sunlight and the fluting of a thousand throats, ringing cello notes, punctuating a chorus that was complex but clear, a miracle of orchestration.

The exhilaration of her dream remained. She flung back the bedclothes and sprang to her feet, her arms thrusting into her robe. Belguardo was calling. She went to the window and leant out. It was a lyrical morning, radiant and cool, light filtering through the crouching shrubs, the sprinkle of dew on the grass and the flowers showing a million diamond facets, dazzling the eye. The whole beautiful scene offered unexpected vistas, the slope of a terrace, a bank of wild orchids, the deliberate profusion of a small grove of South Sea island hibiscus, a flowered curtain of bougainvillea. It was incredibly fresh with the special magic of early morning, the first faint stirrings of the warm, scented earth.

She leaned further out, the very curve of her neck spelling enchantment. It was wonderful to be young and eager, excitement stirring in her. Almost anything could happen on Belguardo. Almost anything *had*! Almost knocking her sideways. Her blood tingled as it had never done before, the slow heat starting at her toes as her vision was assailed by an arrogant dark head, the silver shiver of a light, mocking glance. She blinked it away. It made no sense at all to deliberately court danger. Rian McCallum was outside the limits of her experience and better to remain so.

So close she could almost touch it the silk-cotton tree, a native of Burma, had burst into scarlet blossom, so heavy in nectar it literally spilled to the ground, trailing beauty and the noisy attentions of a dozen or more lorikeets, brilliantly plumaged in enamel colours; emerald and blue and sulphur-yellow. Save for the birds everything was very quiet, very peaceful. Rory wondered if her father's partner had stayed for the night as her father had suggested. Long after she had retired the previous night, the study lights had gone on burning bright into the small hours as the two men discussed the business deal that had never been far from their minds, courteously restrained until the moment she had bade them good night. All through dinner McCallum had never let that smooth mask of urbanity slip for a second, drawing her against her will, whether she liked it or not. Those light eyes were on her profile more times than she cared to think, his dark face faintly saturnine, openly admiring the innocent provocation of the clinging velvet gown, the low oval neckline dipping to the slight shadowed cleft of her breast. It was difficult to retain her poise under that cool, clear glance, so unfairly speculative. Self-interest had never motivated her need to be with her father, but it seemed with his partner she would have to prove it, striking a precarious balance between civility and a carefully concealed antagonism.

65

Anything else would have been to admit total defeat. A shiver started at the bare skin of her nape, swept free of her hair and shuddered down to her feet, not due entirely to the crisp tingle of breeze. Whatever his failings Rian McCallum gripped the imagination, a sure indication that he was a disruptive element in her new-found contentment. For she was content.

In surroundings so different which often tended to change people, she had never experienced a feeling of strangeness, of being a stranger in a strange land. Belguardo was home, she was as certain of this as she was of her own identity. Like an omen, a large butterfly, Chinese blue, mottled with yellow and black on the wing tips, flew by with a dipping languorous grace, then settled like a velvety flower on the windowsill near her hand. It was the final grace.

She turned away, her step lighthearted, searching out saffron coloured slacks and a matching print body shirt, then bent down to the back of the wardrobe to find her sneakers, for she intended to go as far as the canefields; cane that stood twice as high as her head. Twenty minutes later she was walking briskly down the drive, her feet making small crackling sounds on the raked pebbles. She gazed upwards at the feathery poincianas. They would be glorious in October when they began their prolific flowering. All over the plantation, the smaller trees, the frangipani, stood weirdly naked, giving no indication of the beauty, the fragrance, the subtle variation in creamy pastel tints that summer would bring them.

Incredible to think her mother had turned her back on all this, misliking the lush, the exotic, the Capricornian climate, the heat and humidity of the Wet, the incomparable blue and gold of the Dry. It must have been her father's blood calling to her all along. Somehow she must have remembered all this, like a feeling of destiny, this flowering wilderness that was the North, the marvellous texture to the landscape, the colour of the earth and the sky, colour that assaulted the eye.

Alongside her, her mother kept pace with her, a slight dark-eyed ghost, a presence felt but never seen, constantly chiding her for allowing herself to be seduced by the sun country. Her mother would have recoiled into a hard, cold shell if confronted by a man like Rian McCallum. Vivid, vital, demanding men were to be shunned like the plague. In the old days Rory would never have been exposed to a man like that – not if her mother could have helped it.

'And there,' she thought wryly, 'I've done it again. Thought of McCallum!' She resisted the dark distraction he offered, shaking him off with a single-minded determination as she heard in her inner ear, her mother's applause. 'Well done, Rory! Men of charm are invariably vagabonds!'

Clear of the drive, she skirted an expanse of tiny yellow-gold flowers, with a delicious scent, their colour intensified to an extraordinary degree, and stepped delicately around them. She was filled with a wonderful sense of ease, ease of body and mind. She quickened her pace, feeling the soft sigh of the breeze through her hair, reliving in spite of herself a moment when a man's hand had brushed her cheek, the cold certainty of his movements as he caught at the clasp in her hair. Such men were dangerous, for they made a woman deeply conscious of her own femininity, its strengths and its frailties.

To her right lay the pineapple grove and she considered exploring it briefly, but the giant cane drew her like a magnet. Seen close to, it looked very much like bamboo. Spreading fields of it, ripe for the harvest.

Field upon field stretching clear away to the indigo line of the ranges, for unlike the southern areas the cane was unmixed with other crops. North Queensland *was* sugar, practically the only crop that was cultivated and the backbone of primary production.

Rory walked along the red ochre ridges between the giant grasses, looking towards a distant field that lay fallow. The cane took just over a year to mature; irrigation was used wherever possible to speed up the growth of the plant. After harvest, the new cane would be sown by mechanical planter, sending up brilliant new shoots in a very short space of time. Nothing about this season's crop would be wasted. At the mills the sugar would be crushed and the juices concentrated by boiling under pressure until the sugar crystallized out. The fibre would be used for compressed insulating boards, the syrupy mass of molasses for the manufacture of industrial alcohol and rum, the residue for stock feed and fertilizers. It was a totally utilized yield.

Some little way off a cane toad jumped out on the track in front of her and she recoiled with a little *frisson* of fright, amused at her own reaction, considering *her* size and the size of the toad. There were any amount of rustlings in the giant grasses. She turned down the end of the line and walked up another, making back towards the earth road taken by the mighty mechanical harvesters.

Something, a throb of emotion, a faint prickling of the nape, some warning antennae relayed to her that she was being watched. The sugar cane was rustling. She whirled about with a clear and vivid sensation of panic. A new, frightening dimension was introduced into that beautiful scene. Emerging from the tip of the parallel line of cane was a colossus! Not so much in height, though he was tall enough, but in breadth, a grotesquely small head on a thick column of neck, gesticulating towards her, the swarthy face working, shouting something quite incomprehensible, his enormous muscular arms uplifted.

Rory's heart quivered with shock. She could feel herself shrinking, her heart suddenly noisy in her chest. She stared at him, wide-eyed, paralysed by the implications his intimidating appearance presented. She had an irresistible impulse to run, yet she was rooted to the spot. She could never stay and hear him out. His appearance deviated considerably from the normal. Now, all of a sudden, it was unbearably hot and still. An enormous world of silence, green isolation. The colossus started towards her and the instinct for survival took over, operating at full power.

She turned and ran with the swift surefootedness of fear, all the while assailed by an awful vision of attack – pure nightmare out of a green Paradise. She could hear him crashing after her, ludicrously slow with his enormous bulk, and she thanked God for it, almost experiencing a taste of that brutal strength, the swarthy face close to her own. She broke through the green lines of cane, her hair whipping behind her, a young girl with a demon riding her shoulder. Her heart seemed about to burst with the violence of her exercise.

'Rory!'

Her name reached her like the crack of a whip, loud and insistent. She turned her head fractionally, her hair streaking across her cheeks, almost blinding her. It was all over. She was safe. She jerked to a stop, her head drooping, her throat working, trying to subdue the awful accelerated beat of her heart. He reached her in seconds, grasped the soft flesh of her arms and pulled her towards him with the queer glittery look of controlled violence.

69

'Rory!'

His eyes were like silver daggers slashing at her. Her head snapped back on its slender neck. She looked disturbed and disturbing, her own eyes enormous, the pupils dilated, her mouth parted, gasping for breath.

'God in Heaven, what's wrong? What's frightened you like this?'

His hands closed over her collar bones, forcing up her head so that she was left staring into his tautened dark face, the skin polished the colour of resin by the hot sun. She was breathless, watching a muscle jerk beside his mouth. Suddenly she pitched forward.

'Rian!' The husky little cry was torn from her, her glossy, dishevelled head against the smooth-sheened cloth of his shirt. So this was what it was like in the eye of the hurricane, she thought, her mind still confused, her numbed senses reviving. His arms closed about her. Hard. He was dangerous; an unswerving man of ambition, but he was real. So real and important to her survival. She turned her cheek along his hard chest, feeling his heart striking into her own. So long as she stayed where she was, she was safe!

From behind them came the heavy, lumbering steps of her pursuer, his slow, oddly hesitant voice. She burrowed her head still further against McCallum, trembling a little, feeling his hand smooth her hair away from his mouth with a half tender, half impatient gesture. He was speaking now in Italian, a language that was strange to her, his voice carrying a discipline and authority but no vestige of anger. None whatsoever! Not a particle she expected.

He stopped suddenly and looked down at her glistening head. 'Rory! Come on now, you can hear me. So listen. This is Beppo. He was born in this district – we all know him. He wanders at will. I know why you ran,

70

but there was no need to. Beppo's not like the rest of us, but he's completely without vice – gentle, courteous, a good worker, immensely strong. If you look at his eyes they'll reassure you. They are the real Beppo. He was trying to warn you about the snakes. Quite a few of them are sunning themselves along the tracks. They get in the cane, as you know, or *did* you? If you understood Italian you would have grasped what he was trying to say to you. Now look up like a good girl. Beppo will always be around and there's no need to be frightened. He's more upset than you are. Come on, little one, stop burrowing against me, I know you're quite capable of extraordinary things!'

That last little flicker of mockery brought her head up. She turned around in his arms and they fell away from her. Beppo, close to, was scarcely less frightening than he was at a distance but for one thing. His soft dark eyes, with lashes as thick as flue-brushes, held no shade of menace or male speculation or indeed anything but grieved shame. He was quite simply a child who had unintentionally frightened another child and deeply regretted it. The realization cleared her head and steadied her voice.

'I'm sorry, Beppo!' she said, smiling a little sadly, overcome by a sudden wave of pity for this great hulking man-child. 'I didn't realize you were trying to tell me about snakes!'

Behind her, hard at her shoulder, McCallum translated for her, easy and confident and rather freely, she thought, for immediately Beppo was all smiles, bowing and touching his hand to his head. She returned the smile, trying to invest it with as much warmth as she was able after her fright, listening to the soft, liquid spate of conversation between the two men. Beppo saluted and lumbered off, a formidable and unpre-

71

possessing enough sight, but at least he had been explained to her and understanding brought a release from the tremors that were shaking her.

'You might at least applaud my sense of timing!'

She turned to face him, and her mouth quivered at the look on his face.

'I will, when I'm able, Mr. McCallum!'

'So! It was *Rian* a minute ago, but far be it from me to expect consistency in a woman,' he said with silky gentleness. 'But then you're not a woman, just a panicky child!'

She moved her head and her hair fell heavy and shining, flashing out the incipient reds. 'I'm sorry. I made a fool of myself!'

'One might almost wish it on you every day to elicit that kind of response!'

He was laughing a little and she moved uneasily, pretending to shade her eyes from the bright arc of the sun. His eyes were brilliant and mocking, penetrating even when he was at his most casual, which he was now, like a sleek panther, warming himself in full sunlight knowing some form of amusement was well within reach.

'Come on now!' he said softly, 'you're only pretending to be outraged. If you will set out for these early morning jaunts . . . !'

'I wasn't aware that I had to ask permission!' she flashed at him, 'but thank you for rescuing me, Mr. McCallum!'

'*Rian* to you!' he said firmly, his eyes narrowing over her. 'Come to that, I think I agree with you. Why should you toil and spin or anything else you don't care to? You're too beautiful for that. We all capitalize on what assets we've got. One never knows when the years of famine will strike!'

'Somebody should have told me about you!'

'Somebody certainly should have. You can't be too sure of anything in this life, Rory, my girl. A friendly warning!'

His dark face swam above her, coolly ironic, sharpening the pain in her breast. His eyes moved over her leisurely, with mock exasperation.

'You look rather mysterious and a thought too sensitive. Forgive me for laughing at you, but I thought you'd rather die than have me feeling sorry for you!'

His impudence made her physically breathless. 'You're very intelligent indeed!' she said, swinging her head up.

'And now I think you've taken the fantastic notion to dislike me!' His smile tautened. 'Why?'

'I might ask you the same question!'

He was standing very still, his eyes fixed rather broodingly on her. 'My dear child, can't you judge a man by his actions? The odds are, if I *disliked* you as much as you seem to think, you'd have run yourself into the ground by now!'

'It wasn't really worth it, was it?' She gave a funny, helpless little shrug. 'Asking the question!'

'No!' he said gently. 'As things are, it would be very difficult indeed to *like* you, Rory. But tell me about this schoolboy friend of yours. Knowing a little is almost worse than not knowing anything at all!'

She turned on him, her eyes smouldering green fire, dark-fronded brilliance. 'I hope with all my heart that you come a cropper one day!'

'Don't kill all my hopes for us, little one. Hope is such a precious commodity, persisting in the face of every known obstacle!' His eyes looked over her head, coolly detached. 'Don't let's evade the main issue. What's he like, your gentleman suitor?'

'*Human!*' she looked away from him, softly satirical.

'Considerate, sympathetic, sincere!'

'We're all apt to be misjudged!' he commented pleasantly, his arrogant dark head clearly etched against the blue immensity of the sky.

'Well, he *is*!' She swung back to face him, her eyes sparkling defensively.

'No wonder at all you clutch close to him!' He was watching her closely, the mocking twist of his mouth suggesting he could, if he wished, be cruel.

Rory felt a little giddy with all this crazy antagonism. 'Do you always commandeer the conversation like this?' she asked jerkily. 'This dreadful purpose in everything you do!'

He was looking rather lazily down at her, exploring her warmly tinted face, the living light in her hair. 'You're very unusual, Rory!' he murmured conversationally. 'But I think you could, given time, make me very angry indeed. Forgive me for worrying the subject to death, but he works in a bank, doesn't he, your friend?'

He looked the very picture of vivid dark vitality and she was surprised that her voice came out with scarcely a tremor.

'He does, but he doesn't really like it!'

His downbent glance fairly jolted her. 'I thought we might come to that. Life *is* difficult for the working classes!'

She gave him a swift, imploring glance. 'At the risk of repeating myself . . . !'

'. . . you *hate* me! I know. And I hate you too. Now *that*'s over . . . this friend of yours, he's hoping for a position in the Sheridan organization, I take it?'

'You put it so baldly!' Her gaze mingled and darted away from that rapier glance.

'Is there another way?' he inquired, suavely sardonic.

74

'But don't worry so, little one. I quite understand. Most of us have to grab our opportunities. Only the select few have them handed out on a silver platter!'

Her sharp little indrawn breath was quite audible in fraught air. Quick stabbing little darts of anger were piercing her. She couldn't hope to win with him – he had told her as much. She made a jerky little movement away from him, but his lean brown hand descended with enough force on her shoulder to hold her quite still, his dark brows drawing together.

'No, stay right where you are! For one thing I like to retain the initiative and I couldn't bear to watch you take a wrong trail again. After all, I'm only asking you a few simple questions!'

A million prickles ran over her skin. 'An inquisition, you mean!' Desperately she tried to shrug her shoulder away from that hard hand. The mocking quirk to his mouth actually hurt her, yet he had no mercy.

'When do you expect him?' he asked tersely.

'Any day now!' she whispered vehemently. 'We intend to get engaged!'

'Good God!' His hand fell away of its own accord, bringing her futile efforts to an end.

'Now what is that supposed to mean?'

He slanted a silvery glance over her agitated young face. 'A pious wish for your happiness, perhaps. You're madly in love, of course?'

'Would I discuss it with you?' She suddenly put her pale slender fingers to her temples, pressing them hard.

'You wouldn't have to, if you were!' he observed rather curtly. 'I know enough about women to spot a green girl when I see one. And that's a state of affairs that can't last!'

Her voice went tight as if it cost her an effort to get

the words out. 'Why do you treat me like this?'

'How do you want me to treat you?' he asked in a smooth, soothing voice. 'As it is, you're too young to do as I'd like! Come to that, how do you know you're not driving *me* mad?'

'If I could only be certain!' She almost smiled, showing her small even teeth. 'I knew the first moment I laid eye on you that you'd be quite terrifying. Cruel too, like a crouching tiger!'

'And here I was imagining myself a Highland chieftain!' His eyelids dropped, a hint of a laugh in his voice.

'Does Father tell you *everything*?' she asked rather plaintively.

'Poor child! Just about! Enough at any rate to convince me you could wreck this new life of his with a sweep of that auburn head!'

She met the shimmery accusation in his eyes, knowing he was in deadly earnest, as she was herself. 'But I love my father!' she protested. 'I'd never hurt him. Surely you can see that?' His attitude was affecting her deeply, the cynical lights that flickered in the crystal clear depths of his eyes.

'Even if it *was* true,' he cut in on her brutally, 'I've good reason to believe that you could be used as a weapon against his best interests, as women have been used in the past. Rather than let that happen, I'd marry you myself!'

Her mouth parted, pulsing with colour, her heart beating very fast. 'What a magnificent gesture, and so wildly preposterous!' Her eyes were full of brilliant irony, but she didn't move. She couldn't, recognizing that their conversation had moved into a new rather dangerous sphere. She could feel the tension. He lifted his hand and she flung back her head instinctively like a small wild creature sensing the trap.

'Would it be so bad?' he asked, catching the point of her chin, holding her fast. His voice was silky with the merest suggestion of a threat. It licked like wildfire along her veins. She felt burningly alive, all desire to evade him trailing away. He was hypnotizing her and he knew it, a faintly sensual line to his mouth.

'If I didn't know better, I'd think you were no more than a beautiful, underprivileged child. But one day you're going to be a very rich girl as well as a beautiful one, with a lot of the company shares in your hands!'

'You accuse *me* of self-interest! Why, if it bothers *you* so much. . . .' She stopped, staring up at him, warned by the swift, silvery glitter of his eyes, laying herself open to a whole avalanche of complications she couldn't possibly cope with. She could only retreat before a stronger, more ruthless opponent.

'Please, Rian!' Her voice was a ghost whisper that brushed his cheek. She was trembling with dismay and the shivery excitement his touch would always engender in a woman. She forced herself to look into his face – a dark face that made a prisoner of her. It was hard, unforgiving, a forceful, implacable face, and she would never forget it whatever else she forgot.

He released her so abruptly that she experienced a queer sense of vertigo. He seemed to be towering over her, his height and breadth of shoulder never more apparent.

'One of these days, so help me!' he breathed, 'I just might kidnap you for a whole afternoon. A roaring fire of temptation, you might say. But not today! The situation calls for a great deal more finesse!'

Free of him, her courage returned. She could even be herself again. More, quietly sarcastic. 'My greatest ambition is to prove myself to you, Mr. McCallum!'

'In that case relax while you can! It might help you to remember I don't play games, little one. It's time for you to grow up. Nothing is simple or straightforward any more. You've walked right out over the edge of your safe little existence!' His eyes moved over her as if he had every right to such slow deliberation, making a mockery of all her plans. 'Now,' he said lightly, 'let's go back to the house. It's going to be one of those days again. This afternoon I'm taking you across to the island. Your father will be pretty busy for one or two days. We'll stay overnight and bring the family back. Marc, your new stepbrother, should be a push-over!'

CHAPTER FIVE

THE great white sail caught the sun, gleaming like the
snowy underside of a gull's wing; the racing waves
splashed against the stern and a silver glitter of spray
found its way across the bow. It was a sunburst of
beauty, exotic, romantic in the extreme to be skimming
the immensity of the ocean, an intense electric blue, the
coastline vanishing behind them. Alongside hunting
porpoise formed an escort while all about them, seabirds
circled and milled and dropped like stones into the dazzling blue water, rising, glistening with drops of sea
water. The freshening breeze raced off the water,
sweeping the island scents towards them, mingling with
the cooler, salt smell of the sea.

Rory sat very still, feeling the salt breeze whip
through her hair, spilling it around her face in glowing
confusion. It was a warm, sensuous feeling to surrender
herself to the soft magic of sun and water with nothing
to do but envy the sure way McCallum was handling
the boat. He was obviously enjoying himself, nursing
the yacht into the wind, holding her firmly on tack
against a slight buck, the billowing jib giving them a
good two knots better than the diesel engine. The wind
sang in their sails so that they seemed to fly like some
great white bird before the wind.

The lights off the water struck across his dark face,
illuminating, shading, and almost insensibly Rory, in
her mind's eye, found herself sketching his head. The
problem was to capture the complexity of the man, for it
was the dynamic aura he conjured up more clearly than
anything else, that strong dash of sardonic humour. As a

subject she was forced to concede that it was a striking head, almost audacious. No weaknesses. No uncertainties. A taste for challenge and adventure, perhaps? Certainly the unconventional.

He turned his head briefly, disturbing her critical analysis, and she flushed in confusion at the scimitar flash of his eyes. Her own were jade green, still reflecting an objective response to vivid male beauty. Or so she imagined. Whatever it was McCallum didn't see it that way. A rather raffish look crossed his dark face, deepening the curve of his mouth.

'In anyone else, I'd take *that* as an obvious invitation!' Her skin tightened electrically. She tried desperately to emulate his ease and sophistication, a little hammer going at the base of her throat.

'I'm so glad you realize it was no such thing!'

'Which just goes to prove a theory of mine. True seduction is born in a woman, never assumed. Yours was handed out in the cradle!' His cool, level gaze was devastating. He turned back to the wheel. 'What were you doing anyway? Compiling a dossier – complete to the last detail?'

Her eyes fixed themselves on a point between his wide shoulders. 'You wouldn't believe me if I told you!'

'Try me!'

'I was mentally sketching your head!'

'Good God!' There was a mocking, amused timbre in his dark, resonant voice.

'You don't have to make it sound . . . *eccentric*!'

'Forgive me!' His glance slid over her gently. 'Tell me, are you any good?'

'You can judge for yourself. At a much later date!' She glanced at him fleetingly and away again. It seemed much safer that way. 'You don't like women, do you,

Mr. McCallum?'

'Rian, in emergencies only! Let's say, honey, not deep down!' He studied her face, disturbed, tinted like a ruffled flower. 'When you colour like that I find myself remembering your father's claims.'

'Oh?' The sheer element of wanting to know made her look into his face, dispelling caution.

His eyes gleamed, his mouth twisted with faint irony. 'I'm not sure if he doesn't rate you the most fabulous young creature ever born!'

'I'll learn!' she said wryly, falling into the trap. 'Or better still, carefully refrain from asking you any more questions!'

The air seemed suddenly static, like the lull before the storm. It was the gravest error to cross swords with McCallum. She twisted her head away. He was too tall, too lithe, too purposeful! He flickered a glance over her averted profile, a pure silhouette against the blue sky.

'Now that's what makes women more interesting than men at any rate! They're so damned moody!'

'I am not!' She turned her head back, quickly protesting.

'*And* they will persist in taking every last word ... personally!'

She had the grace to smile. 'That I can't deny. It seems I've struck a rich vein of philosophy. A bachelor's philosophy!'

'Of course! Half of us are ruthless, little one. The other half henpecked! However, when one comes right down to it, women are the real dictators. God – power! They get drunk on it!'

'You shock me!' she said, the expression on her face making the comment superfluous.

'I'm sorry!' he inclined his dark head sardonically. 'Far be it from me to topple your girlish fantasies.

81

You're right at the age when pretty myths outweigh the hard facts. To the innocent everything's possible! Roses all the way. Only experience teaches us otherwise. But never mind, it's wonderful while it lasts!' He flung her a glance that made her want to break out in open mutiny.

'You're a mocking devil, Rian McCallum!' she said softly.

'You floor me! However, it's been said before. Mostly by your own sweetly unscrupulous sex. You can't all be wrong!' His voice turned sharply indulgent. 'Don't tilt that chin at me. It's all wasted. You're no more than a fleecy white lamb let loose with a wolf pack!'

Inexplicably his voice had a ring of sincerity. It disconcerted her thoroughly. 'I can't believe that. I *won't* believe it!'

'You'll have to!' he laughed gently. 'I even have it in my heart to feel sorry for you!'

She stared at him almost compulsively. 'Well, that's one solitary fragment of comfort. But please don't let's waste a wonderful trip striking sparks off each other!'

'What would you suggest?' His brilliant light eyes travelled over her and the shock to her heart was sudden, constricting. It tempered her voice, shaken, a little breathless.

'Do you know you actually make me feel nervous!'

'Well, it's damned well time!' He let out his breath in mock disappointment. 'What an anti-climax! For a moment there, I thought you might be serious. Failing that, why don't you tell me about when you were a little girl?'

'Surely you're not interested?'

His dark brows shot up in denial. 'My dear child, the sooner I know all about you, the better! Now tell me, that's an order and we're way out to sea!'

Against her will, she responded while he looked straight ahead at a glorious seascape emblazoned in the sun. Somehow she found herself telling him a great deal more than she intended, only to wonder that same night when sleep didn't come easily . . . *why*? She had not said nearly so much to her father. Certainly not Kim. Perhaps it was the effect of the sun on the water – narcotic, the air tangy, whipping away inhibitions. He didn't interrupt and it was a masterly touch. She knew this, but it didn't dam the quick flow of words. He was too clever a hand. Only once when she faltered, he coaxed her along with a softly intent:

'*Tell* me!'

So she did. She told him how, when she was a child, she cried herself to sleep many nights, willing her life to be different. The memory still caused her pain, a faint twinge of the old desperations, the sense of guilt, the imagined disloyalties to her mother, the empty loneliness for an imaginative, alert and sensitive child. The times when her mother's cold silence persisted for days. The times they quarrelled – not often, but bitterly. And always about her father.

'*Man's ingratitude to women!*' It had been one of her mother's favourite themes. She stopped on a wave of feeling. Her throat rippled, a rapid, instinctive thing, her head tilted back, the sun gilding her eyes and her skin, the gleaming, heavy fall of her hair.

He shot her a quick look, molten silver, very hard to define.

'You're a vulnerable young creature, Rory. It wasn't much fun!' His voice was quiet, matter-of-fact, asking nothing.

'It was the song of my life. Not so sad. In some ways a lot better than most!'

'You're wrong there, little one.' His fingers steadied

83

the wheel. 'A child can well do without luxuries. They're hardly aware of them in any case. What they can't do without is the right kind of loving. That's a fierce necessity, otherwise it comes against them, one way or the other!'

She gave a soft little sigh of agreement, arching her back a little against the bunk like a small feline creature smoothing her fallen hair. The segment of sun made its highlights glitter and dance like rubies. 'I know I've been too serious with you and I shall never, never be so serious again!'

He only smiled and made no answer. She felt oddly defenceless watching him standing there, wide-shouldered, lean-hipped, his dark head thrown up, eyes narrowed against the dazzle of sunlight. The man, the sea of incredible beauty, the wild, untamed sound of the birds, all blended together into one single entity. Somehow she had the feeling it would always be so. The thought disturbed her, filling her with a brittle kind of energy. She swung to her feet and came to stand beside him, making herself look up into that dominant dark face.

'It's all so very beautiful, isn't it? Is this my father's yacht?'

'No, it isn't, my sweet little innocent!' He glanced down his straight nose at her, his eyes brilliantly mocking. 'It's mine! And you're on it!'

'Well, I was hardly to know that, was I? I mean, all you and Father said was *the boat*. It could have been anyone's boat!' Something about his expression made her feel utterly ridiculous.

'If anyone has a chance, Rory, you have!'

She looked up at him quickly, trying to gauge the odd note in his voice. 'You're a bit edgy today, aren't you?'

84

'We're all a bit edgy!' he agreed, more amused than perturbed.

'You're right about that and wrong about everything else!' she murmured laconically.

His eyes slipped over her downbent head, the heavy sweep of her lashes. 'No man is infallible, my child!' In front of the beautifully flared bows, the sea shone like shot silk, overlaid with a luminous veil of silver, the yacht riding the swells so that it seemed they were alone in a world of light and movement, the breeze whipping up excitement and enthusiasm.

'I wish I could handle a boat,' she said warmly.

He smiled a little at her tone. 'I'll teach you.'

She swung her bright head back to him. 'That's a piece of altruism I deeply appreciate!'

'Oh, Rory,' he mocked her, 'how can we possibly share a friendship if you insist on using those sharp little barbs against me?'

'Perhaps we can arrive at some compromise solution,' she suggested, sweetly reasonable. 'I already have a friendship!'

One dark eyebrow flared. 'How could I ever forget? What was the name again?'

'I'm sure Father told you!'

His eyes gleamed with the old, customary arrogance. 'He did – Kim, Kim Barrett. Tell me, how long have you known him?'

She watched, not his face, but his lean brown hands on the wheel. 'A little over a year.'

'He must possess considerable restraint!' The light malice in his voice was barely concealed.

'I don't follow you.'

'No!' He flickered her a crooked little smile, satirical, a shade curt. 'Your mother approved, I take it?'

'She did!' Almost unknown to her her hand was

85

clenching and unclenching and he smiled at the violent, compulsive little movement.

'You wouldn't be satisfied with friendship, my girl, if you'd ever had love!'

'I'm *in* love!' She stared back at him, wholly unprepared for the swift arrogant charm of his smile.

'A lovely thought and thank you for sharing your secret!'

She gave a curious, rapid shake of her head. 'What a tease you are!'

'What a stickler *you* are! So scornful and denying. Don't be so sure you know so much about love, and don't get confused between what you feel and what you think you *ought* to feel. Nothing's carved out to a nicety, little one!'

'I know!'

'You do? Then take that sad look off your face. A man could go crazy just chasing your expressions!'

It was very difficult not to respond to the glint of amusement in his eyes. 'I like you too!' she said carelessly.

'What eloquence!' he gave a little twist of a smile, the hard, self-contained look back on his face again.

She went to the wheelhouse window and looked out. 'You know, it's the strangest thing, but you make me feel a usurper. The stand-in stealing the leading role!'

He gave a brief laugh. 'What fanciful nonsense!'

'Perhaps the family will feel the same way?' she persisted.

His voice was tersely emphatic. 'You're taking nothing away from them that belongs to them. Just remember that!'

She swung back to stare at him, a faintly perplexed look in her eyes.

'Just whose side are you on, McCallum?'

There was a silence and all of a sudden he reached for her, a lightning gesture, one hand twitching the wheel, the other curved over the point of her shoulder:

'Who said you could call me McCallum? Rian to you, you green-eyed, disrespectful brat!'

She trembled a little, a dreamlike expression in her eyes. 'Do you really think they'll like me?'

His hand shifted. With his fingers he tilted up her chin, an odd light in the depths of his eyes.

'Relax, can't you? No one is going to offer the slightest resistance to Bren's little girl-child. Not while I'm around!'

She was shaken by the implacable set of his head, the shivery feeling of his skin on hers. 'Is that your prerogative, then? Don't do as *I* do . . . !'

'Something like that.' He released her with a careless gesture, a man, masterful and confident. 'Don't worry, little one, your life is only beginning. Up here you'll have to unfurl all those tight creamy petals, accept the demands a full life will make upon you, for it's all useless repetition without fresh experience.'

The boat suddenly swam into a long trough, upsetting her balance and causing her to slide sideways. His arm caught her up, hauling her close up against him, his dark face taut and wary. In that little eye of quiet, the incredibly bright seascape was hazy and uncertain. His image possessed her mind, his dark head blocking out the barbaric white gold of the sun. Unconsciously she turned up her face to him, her eyes enormous, intense, shimmering like emeralds. Something very strange was happening to her, a white-hot flame, relentless and fierce licking along her veins. . . .

His voice flicked at her like the touch of a whip. 'Don't start making difficulties. Not now. This minute!'

87

Her breath caught in her throat. 'Let me go!'

'Why, certainly, my lady. The only brave thing I've ever done!'

Her face was burning under that glance of natural, mocking candour, aching for the cooling touch of the breeze.

'The wonder is you don't throw me in!' she said in a rush, almost recklessly.

He gave a great peal of laughter. 'I assure you I don't abandon my responsibilities so lightly!'

'And that's what I am? A responsibility?'

'It will do for a start!' he commented dryly. 'Don't fret, my lamb, I won't expect much. Just blind obedience!' He sketched her a sardonic smile, but she evaded his eyes as if they were a silver trap, the wild rose colour suffusing her skin. Everything about him, the imperious tilt of his head the angle of his shoulders, the deep cleft of his chin, was frankly, vibrantly male. It was inevitable that he would antagonize women. Yet in a curious fashion her eyes gravitated back to him throughout the ensuring silence.

He smiled a little ironically at her tangible air of hostility and began to tell her about the Reef, a tutor to a bright child, immensely informative, but definitely intent on keeping her in her place. All the same, she listened, caught up in the web of fact and legend, the beauty and wealth of the marine life that was one of his special interests. He knew the Reef waters well, as a yachtsman and a scuba diver, claiming that the green silent world of the deeps was fantastically beautiful, a perfect microcosm of the brilliant and abundant life of the coral seas. Soft sea grasses gold and green and deep rose swaying gently as if to a breeze; the sculptured beauty of the coral flowers in their immense gardens; the giant anemones spreading their tentacles like so many petals; the shoals of gorgeous little fish that made a riotous wave of colour in those primeval underwater forests; no weight of the body, just liquid motions of the limbs, man perfectly happy out of his habitat.

Rory stared at his dark profile, the gleaming, illuminating smile. He baffled and excited her. There was something about him suggestive of his whole background; the Reef and the blue sea, the rain forest, the shimmering savannahs visited by the monsoon, a quality of vitality of vivid, dark energy and strength. It came to her then that he was in many ways like her father – or as her father had been years before with the thrusting ambition that had sent him on his way. Perhaps it was as her mother had always said, men who excited you and swept you up in their path would only end by destroying you and all chance of happiness. Her mother had lived out her own contention. Perhaps it *was* true. She only knew that at the moment Rian McCallum had her playing inexorably into his hands.

He looked across at her and caught the strange expression in her brilliantly green eyes.

'Let me in on all those despairing glances. What do they mean?'

For a single, burning instant she had the irresistible impulse to tell him. But the instant passed.

'All right,' he said softly, '*don't* tell me! And I thought this was a pleasure trip!' There was a still, shining light in his striking eyes and still she did not speak, believing he could almost read her mind. Her heart seemed to be beating loudly in the stillness and the only reality was the man who was regarding her so straightly. She turned her head away abruptly, catching her breath, looking into the crystal abyss of the deep ocean. Some latent effects of her mother's influence still endured in her. The kindest thing Rian McCallum could do for her would be to ignore her. The worldly and the experienced had a powerful fascination for novitiates. She would be a fool to deny the sensuous effect the sight and the sound of him had on her. Her green eyes sparkled with a kind of self-contempt. She shook back her hair, letting the sun warm her, dismissing the man from her mind. Not for anything would she admit final defeat. He stood before the wheel, tall and relaxed, a faintly derisive smile on his mouth. Rory fastened her eyes on the horizon.

Forty minutes later they raised the island. Sorella! It grew like a misty sketch on the shining rim of the ocean to an emerald diadem, ringed by blinding white sand with tall fringing hoop pines standing against the sky, a white ruffle of surf sparkling against the niggerheads. Sorella! One of the hundreds of islets of the Great Barrier Reef Channel, some true coral islands, rising like magic from the sea floor, others, continental islands, isolated relics of high land, once part of the Queensland mainland. All of them fabulously beautiful, sprinkled like gemstones along the mighty coral rampart that followed the coastline for over twelve hundred miles.

Rory felt the warmth and excitement whip into her veins. There was something in the psychology of man that drew them towards coral islands; artists and authors and scientists alike lured by their beauty and exotica, their mystery and wealth of scientific data and puzzles. She turned her head swiftly on a wave of enthusiasm.

'Rian!'

'Hmmm!' he smiled at the soft little lilt she gave to his name.

'It's exciting, isn't it? I've never seen the islands, the Reef. There are so many things I've got to do – go fossicking on the inshore reef at low water, explore the coral gardens, swim, get a tan – and I *do* tan, believe it or not!'

'I *have* noticed the spectacular lack of freckles,' he said in a light teasing tone.

'I hope the family like me. Tell me about Leonora?'

'What is it you want to know?' he turned his dark head carelessly. 'She's handsome. She's stylish. A good hostess, a devoted mother.'

'And a wife?'

His eyes flicked her lightly. 'Come on now, green eyes, we'll have to skitter around that one, as well you know!'

'Do *you* like her?'

'*Rory!*'

One glance was enough to tell her she wasn't going to get any more out of him. She crossed her slender arms in front of her in a self-protective fashion.

'I tell you everything and you tell me nothing! Is that it?'

'I'll tell you *one* thing,' he offered without hesitation. 'In among their Latin good looks you're going to be a very exotic butterfly indeed. In fact you'll provide the perfect foil for Tonia!'

'Who loves you dearly, I don't doubt!'

'Now what are you on about?' The sun seared his dark face and he looked hard and dangerous and a complete stranger.

She turned up a face of utter bewilderment, perplexed by the sudden shift in his manner. 'I made it up this very minute!'

His eyes dwelt on her for a few interminable minutes, then he smiled, a shade sharply: 'Well, that's all right, then!'

She couldn't restrain herself, not if her life depended

upon it. 'Why, you're as frightened of entanglements as I am!'

'A profound observation!' he said very dryly. 'Especially for a girl who so sweetly declared herself to be in love. The thing is, Rory, you don't look for it. You don't *want* it, but there it is. The one thing you haven't calculated on, and not much you can do about it. Just another helpless victim in the grip of a headlong emotion. You can't begin to explain it. The way a woman looks is only the half of it. It's more an innate recognition – on both sides!'

There was a faintly intense slant to the line of her brows. 'You seem to know a great deal about it!'

His eyes touched her lightly. 'Beneath this hard exterior which appears to disturb you, there beats an idealistic heart! Besides, little one, I've had my few straying fancies. Every man does, though I can't say I approve of them in women.'

'Indeed no!' She sat down again, locking her hands. 'A man has every right to be promiscuous, a woman, never!'

'That's how it is, green eyes. A provoking problem, I grant you!'

Her glance lifted, studying him intently, with inexhaustible patience. He turned his head abruptly, catching her eyes, wide and unguarded.

'You seem to be testing me all the time, Rory, against some inner standard, not necessarily your own. Your mother wouldn't have approved of me!'

'I know!'

His sudden laugh, like a deep bell in his throat, made her shake her head in confusion. 'I'm sorry, I suppose I shouldn't have been so blunt!'

'It's not in the usual run of polite conversation,' he agreed idly, his eyes mocking her, branding her a graceless adolescent. When he spoke again his voice had turned to crisp decisiveness. 'For every door that shuts, a new one opens. Sometimes it hurts to even draw breath. But the narrow, the confined, the rigid existence is not for you. Before you're very much older you're going to find out what it's like to be really alive . . . the bud turning into the flower.'

The sun struck obliquely across the side of his head, turning his skin to copper. He gave the impression of great vigour and what she construed to herself as ruthlessness. The words were drawn from her, softly, very serious.

'You rather frighten me, Rian!'

'It's the truth that's frightening you!' he amended rather curtly, and turned away from the vivid clear green of her eyes.

For the first time in her life she was emotionally disturbed by a man. Not any man – McCallum! With all the terrible implications for herself. Even in repose, a faintly cynical line to his mouth, he was an extremely handsome man, sombre, a little hard, arrogant eyes and mouth. The hard-headed Scot with plenty of respect for money, yet he had this strange immovable power, some mysterious force that seemed to reach out for her like an invisible current. As if to confirm it he glanced abruptly over his shoulder, drawn by the vibrations of her slightly trembling body.

'Now what is it? You look like a harried child. Extraordinarily tragic!'

There was an ironic light in his eyes that made her bend her head forward, her body curving sideways on its narrow waist, her voice low and economical. 'Perhaps I was considering the tenet: Love thine enemy!'

Instantly there was a wicked gleam in his eyes like the flash of sun on ice. 'There's no hard and fast rule about that, *poverina*! It would be a damned sight easier not to make an enemy of me at all!'

She gave all her attention to the fast growing island, deliberately changing the subject. '*Poverina*? what does that mean? Poor child, something like that? I'll have to take up Italian, I can see. I've only the usual smattering of French and German.'

His eyes glinted, for the moment malicious, moving over her face in the brilliant flood of sunlight.

'I'm sure Marc won't shirk that very pleasant task. Now sit back and don't talk to me for the next ten minutes or so. I need to concentrate from now on. The channel runs fast and narrow.'

She was shocked into disobedience. 'Surely you're not going to take her in under sail?'

'Sit still!' He heard the note in her voice, but he was clearly unrepentant, very masculine, very preoccupied, his eyes full of a bright challenge.

Rory sat back, locking her arms around her knees. She knew she should be filled with a great anxiety, but strangely she couldn't summon up any such notion.

Dead ahead was the island, a ring-shaped scrap of land, floating in the shining, emerald stillness of the enclosed lagoon. Outside its encircling reef, the surf shot mounting crests of spray, iridescent in the sun, like a peacock's tail. On the parched ivory of the coral strand a kingfisher suddenly flashed up and soared away like a blue flame. The long swells were growing deeper now as the sea floor grew shallow near the reef and the racing white-capped waves lifted the stern of the long elegant craft.

A hundred yards from the reef, braced, his head thrown back, McCallum lined the yacht up with the high twisted arches of a pandanus that overshot the beach on its western point, then he set the yacht at a rush for the entrance. Rory shut her eyes, overawed by the clamour of the fast-running narrows, the swirling eddies of blue ocean. When she opened them again they were sailing serenely over the lakelike placidity of the lagoon shining like a sheet of glass, shot through now with opal colours reflecting the enchanted world of the coral meads and grottoes.

She raced to the side of the boat, entranced, while the white sails rattled to the decks. Rian went past her swiftly, competently, to let go the anchor. When finally all was ready, he came back to her and pointed to the blazing line of the beach, the palms that bent their heads to the direction of the wind.

'We'll take the outboard in. Marc's spotted us already.'

The dull echo of a shout reached them from the beach. A young man raced along the sand, ran splashing through the shallows, then struck out in a powerful overarm towards the yacht. The sand was so brilliantly white it hurt Rory's eyes. Rian glanced down at her profile, suddenly very brisk.

'Right-oh, collect your gear. I'll lower the dinghy over the side.'

She waited for no more but raced down to the cabin to collect her small overnight bag, conscious of a rising nervous tension. Now she was here, she was uncertain of her reception. A few minutes later they were tearing away towards the sun-drenched island, hearing the shouts of welcome drift across the water. She gazed at Rian, only to find him watching her with alive, interested eyes.

'Every man, woman and child carries their burden of anxieties, little one. Try to relax. As you can see, Marc is about to make his precipitate entrance!'

They were nearing the shore and he turned and

switched off the motor, letting the dinghy slide into the shallows. Marc was upon them, the salt water glistening all over his face, his black-lustred head, the deeply tanned body. He grasped the side of the dinghy with quick determination.

'Well now, here we are!' His voice was only very faintly accented, warmly exuberant, his large dark eyes even more so. 'A great big today! A pearl of a day! *Va bene, fratellino mio?*' He addressed himself to Rian, but his eyes were all for Rory's subtle smile.

McCallum looked more than ever sardonic, his light eyes gleaming. '*Benissimo*, Marco! But introductions can wait until we beach this thing. *Andiamo, amico!*'

Marc smiled broadly, his eyes so dark the iris and pupil seemed one. 'But I can see for myself, this is my so beautiful stepsister. *Ma che bella signorina! Bella, bellissima!*'

'She does understand *some* Italian!' Rian remarked very dryly. He suddenly swooped forward like a hawk and lifted Rory high in his arms, waded through the shallows to the beach, leaving Marc to drag the dinghy in after them.

'But I shall store this moment away in my senses. For ever!' Marc called after them, in no way disconcerted as Rory undoubtedly was, her heart knocking against her ribs, colour flooding her satiny smooth skin. McCallum was looking down at her with an oddly detached curiosity, the expression around his eyes sharply drawn and definite. God, what an unpredictable man! She fastened her eyes on Marc's brown, compact body as a form of relief.

'So romantic an entry, enchanted my dear friend, one finds oneself enslaved to such things!' Marc was still rhapsodizing.

'So much the worse for accuracy!' McCallum said

briefly.

'But let me finish, *per piciare*, please, my temperament . . . !'

'Come on now, *amico*, don't overburden yourself. Rory, this is Marc, of course. He has a very simple classifying system with women. Either they're *bella* or they're not!'

Rory held out her hand smiling and Marc carried it to his lips with unaffected aplomb, a true Latin, with a zestful and unabashed eye for a good-looking woman. Despite the explicit glances Rory was unperturbed, smiling, looking into his eyes to return his greeting.

'I'm so glad to meet you at last, Marc. I hope we'll be friends!'

'*Friends? Dio mio!* What complications! With a mouth so exquisite. Your beauty, *cara mia*, is increasing by the minute. That smooth heavy hair! Such a colour. What eyes! Strange eyes, I think, luminous around the pupil. The pupil is dilating a little . . . !'

'. . . I don't wonder,' McCallum cut in dryly. 'Rory wasn't expecting such a particularly tempestuous scene. A veritable *Traviata*!'

Marc continued to hold Rory's hand, peering through his heavy lashes into her face.

'*Mi dispiace molto!* I'm so sorry! Can I be blamed, *cara*, if I like looking at you? You are beautiful. It is not necessary for you to talk to me!'

'At this point we find ourselves up against an insurmountable wall. Rory, dear girl, shall we proceed up the beach?' McCallum swung on her, very tall, very sardonic, the only adult on the scene.

Marc spread his hands. 'An arrogant devil, isn't he? But *so* necessary. Still, I have no desire to cross him. Come, *piccola*, my mother and Tonia must meet you. You will forgive Tonia if she sees you second. Cal, you understand, wears a halo round his head. What is it, the knight in shining armour?'

Rian dropped a heavy hand on the younger man's shoulder, causing him to wince slightly: 'That's what I like about you, Marco, your simple lack of restraint. Rory, for one, won't understand Tonia's quaint vision. It's far too civilized for her. She's drawn towards the primitive!'

Marc grasped the soft flesh of Rory's upper arm. 'You are, my beautiful one! Such radiance I see before us!'

'And now's the time to tell him, little one, about . . . Kim!'

'Kim?' Marc's quick exclamation made the name sound ludicrous. 'Who is this Kim? Man or woman? Don't tell me, I know. You can't be serious, *bella mia*, give yourself a little time to reach a true understanding of your fate!'

McCallum suddenly broke into a laugh that had the true ring of amusement. 'For once, I agree with you. Such clearsightedness is always appealing!'

Rory walked between them in the white-gold sunshine, countless details crowding into her mind. Two men, so different. One so cool and sardonic, the other laughing, looking into her face impervious to rebuke. The beauty of the lagoon was incredible, its colour and clarity jade green where it broke on to the dazzling sands. Pandanus and coconut palms lined the shore and countless hibiscus, oleanders, jasmine, ginger blossom and sweet gardenia spiked the air and stirred the senses with their flaunting tropic beauty.

Up from the beach rose a canopy of pisonia trees where the noddy terns nested and chattered, a cool green haven filtered by a lovely soft flood of light. They walked towards it and Rory could see the house, white and beckoning. The whole front was opened up by sliding glass doors and fixed panels to the beautiful scene, protected by a deep cool overhang and sun deck. A climbing allamanda adorned its posts and beams with yellow-gold trumpets so that the house had a clean open aspect like some beautiful spacious greenhouse.

Just as they reached the coral path that led to the house, a girl darted through the open glass doors, her voice thrilling with pleasure.

'Cal!'

'What else is new?' her brother observed laconically, watching his sister's flying figure with a dispassionate eye. She came on towards them like a gazelle, very pretty, very vivacious, a short sheer jacket flying over a brief two-piece swimsuit, her body tanned to a dark gold. She was small, rather distractingly curvy, but with a very small waist. Her resemblance to her brother was quite striking, her hair curling in graduated lengths with the sheen of black satin, her dark eyes sparkling with immense élan.

'Cal! *E vero!* It's true I couldn't believe it!'

Rian advanced a few unhurried paces to meet her and Marc turned his dark head to Rory, his voice dropping to a confidential level.

'Enter my sister in the flower of her youth and precious little else! But who can blame her when she sees the one she loves best in all the world. But *che t' accadde*? What's the matter, *piccola*? You've lost a little of that lovely colour!'

She glanced at him smilingly, her eyes black-lashed, iridescent. 'Why, nothing. Marc. I'm nervous. I suppose. This is quite a day for me – meeting my father's family for the first time!'

'*Si!*' Marc looked thoughtful, then turned away with one lithe gesture to pluck a ruffled hibiscus in a deep orange gold and push it through Rory's hair. '*Per voi*! for you, little sister. May your beauty shine before you on this island paradise!' His black eyes glinted with admiration, his eyes on the texture of skin and flower. 'Your pleasure on meeting is as nothing compared to mine!'

A few pebbles flew and Tonia came down on them at a rush while Rian continued up to the house with Rory's overnight bag. Tonia landed beside them holding out her hand.

'Rory, forgive me! It's a great joy for us to welcome you among us. No stuffy introductions, please. I am Tonia. We are of an age and we shall be friends. But you're like a painting, so still and serene. *Una gioia improvvisa?* A happy surprise, eh, Marco?' She leaned forward and touched Rory's cheek with her smooth rosy lips. 'Mamma is dressing. You will excuse her for the moment. We were not prepared, you understand. Mamma never likes to be caught unawares. We will all have a long cool drink on the deck while we wait. I'm so very glad Cal brought you across. I haven't seen him for ... for ... oh, such a long time!' She took a deep theatrical breath which was, nevertheless, entirely natural.

'Three weeks, my angel?' her brother inquired with faint sarcasm.

Tonia laughed and brushed back her hair. 'Take no notice of him. He is a devil and he will try to make love to you at the first opportunity!' The lustrous black eyes sharpened to the most acute interest. 'You have an admirer, Rory?'

'There is someone, yes,' Rory volunteered with a smile, not nearly so completely as Tonia would have wished. 'I hope you will meet him very soon.'

'We shall be delighted,' Tonia responded with considerable largesse, not the least self-conscious of the considerable smooth areas of skin she was exposing. 'One might have known such a beautiful, reserved girl would be making marriage plans!'

Marc burst into a hiccough of laughter. 'Did you really say that, *cara mia*? To my ears you said nothing about *marriage*!'

'We shall see!' Tonia was smiling, unconcerned, looking at Rory with approval. 'It is after all what a woman dreams about – desiring to be desired by a man. *The* man. Marriage. Children. Long golden days of happiness. Long nights of passion!'

Marc gave a great groan in his throat. '*Gran Dio!* Embarrassing, isn't she? But she can't help it, poor child. It is her nature!'

'And yours!' They turned to each other, brother and sister, showing their tensions in the same way.

'Rian wants us,' Rory said in a calm soothing voice.

Tonia turned on her instantly. 'Rian? You call him Rian? I have not heard this. We all call him Cal! He prefers this, you know.'

In that case I'll continue to call him Rian! Rory thought inwardly, but continued to smile into Tonia's sparkling eyes, coal black like her brother's. As long as she showed no interest in Rian McCallum she would have Tonia for a friend.

It was while they were sitting out on the sun deck overlooking the lagoon that Leonora Sheridan came through to them, her sophisticated gaze travelling over each face in turn, taking in Rory's slender fragility, her lovely colouring, placing her resemblance to her father at once. She was smiling her greetings, accepting Rian's suave comments with enchanting grace, the great calm and composure of the born beauty.

Certain women, Rory reflected, would always defy time, and Leonora was one of them. Her beauty was of the night, dark and languorous. Her features were carved like those of a Roman goddess, in the heroic vein as was her beautiful Junoesque figure. Her nose was very slender, her mouth full, a lovely curve to her brow and chin. She bore no particular resemblance to either of her two children apart from a racial one. She walked towards Rory with a regal movement of her body, her long patio gown moulding the line of her thighs, giving an impression of tremendous calm without being in the least inflexible.

The girl was standing and she took her two hands. 'You are very like your father!' she said at last in a voice as rich and flowing as run honey, then she bent and kissed Rory's cheeks with the full mouth so like painted petals.

'Thank you, *signora*.' Rory gazed intently into the night-dark eyes that were so curiously unrevealing. 'I have never reconciled myself to being without him!'

Leonora raised her fine brows quickly. 'There never was and never will be a Utopia, *cara*. We must take life as we find it and sometimes if we are lucky our dreams come true. We must make you as happy as possible!'

She looked over the lovely curve of her shoulder to Rian. The creamy lids fell, but not before Rory saw lights in those dark eyes like sparks shooting from a hidden and smouldering fire. 'We shall have a party tonight, *caro*, do you think so? To welcome Rory.'

'It sounds very agreeable!' he murmured lazily, his whole posture one of lithe relaxation.

'We go to Belguardo tomorrow?' she asked him.

'When you're ready!' he amended with smooth courtesy, having every intention of leaving at the appointed time, as they all very well knew.

'I'm ready, *caro*.' Leonora smiled her enigmatic smile. 'More than ready! Tell me, child, what do you think of my son . . . my daughter? Are they not beautiful as you are yourself, but in a different manner?' Her eyes rested on Marc and Tonia, the two smiling faces upturned to her, and her own face was transfigured by a tenderness and an indomitable devotion that moved Rory and made her feel faintly uneasy, though she knew it was only a manifestation of a powerful law of nature. Some irresistible force made her search out a pair of light eyes, cool and insistent under their lifted dark brows. He was looking right at her, his expression inscrutable.

Rory eased back into the shade, the forgotten hibiscus flower a counterfoil to the rich red of her hair. Her green eyes were glowing like jewels, debating in her own mind one or two things, peculiar and original. Leonora was addressing her and she came out of her odd reverie.

'You are new to all this, *cara* – the Reef, the islands, our luminous green canefields?'

Rory looked across into that patrician, rather impassive face and nodded her head. 'Coming across from the mainland I thought I'd seen all there was to see of beauty. There's something incomparable about seascapes, the eternal fascination of water. The silver wake curving behind us and before us the great sapphire sweep of the ocean, the air as fresh as the first dawn!'

Leonora inclined her black satin head with approval. 'You have a receptive nature, my child. It would do you good to travel. Your father may go abroad this year. Is that not so, *caro*?' She looked towards Rian and the sun slid across her thick magnolia skin.

'It's possible!' McCallum conceded politely, 'but I hardly think probable, Leonora. We've much too much lined up, you know!'

'So!' Leonora looked down at her beautiful strong hands, the great emerald cut diamond that struck at the eyes. 'My husband rarely discusses his business life with me. In fact, *caro*, he virtually keeps himself hidden from everyone but you!'

'I'm sorry!' That dark vibrant voice cut through a network of hidden tensions. 'Let me put it another way. Bren's a very prominent man. He has many demands on his time and he holds a number of directorships. You could say he's besieged from any number of quarters. I can only do so much myself. It's not easy, my dear!'

Tonia made a distraction, her melting dark eyes on her mother's full, flawless profile.

'I hope we won't be losing, Rory, now that we have found her, Mamma. She is to be married soon.'

Leonora looked closely at her daughter. '*Che mai dite?* What are you saying, Antonia? Is this true, *cara*?' She directed her dark gaze at Rory, who moved a little warily as if a trap was already closing about her.

'We're all embarrassing the child!' McCallum inserted deftly, not giving her the opportunity to speak. 'The fact is, she's not even engaged!'

'*O, gioia*, I'm coming back to life! See, Mamma!' Marc fell back on his upholstered couch, lifting his arms skywards. 'Reborn, reborn! I feel a new strength. Not even engaged!'

His mother smiled at him with great affection, her great eyes worldly wise and serene. 'You appear to have already broken my son's heart, Rory. However, Marco my darling, let me remind you not to be too premature. Rory must take her time. She is very young. One must be sure. Naturally she must invite anyone she wishes to Belguardo and to the island, of course. We shall undertake to make them very welcome. And now, my children, as we must leave in the morning, you must show

104

Rory the reef. She may wish to swim in the lagoon. Go exploring before the light fails. There will be many other opportunities for you to enjoy the island, *cara*, but for now, Cal and I have a few matters to discuss and then I shall give orders for dinner. You like lobster, my child? Such magnificent specimens Marco has been bringing in lately. You must leave it all to me. I shall arrange a festive dinner in honour of your return!'

Rory stood up, very young, very slender, the sun flashing out all the reds of her hair. 'You're very kind to me, *signora*!'

Leonora rose to her feet also, holding up a beautiful imperious hand. '*Leonora*, please, little one. I could not wish for more!'

'*Leonora!*' Rory repeated, knowing herself no match for this tall and benign goddess.

CHAPTER SIX

THE firing began at sunset and would last throughout the night. The flames leapt in the distance, a red-gold holocaust, a fantasy inferno, against the black velvet sky. Rory turned away from the window to resume dressing. Her father was giving a small dinner party, a combination of business and pleasure, and the firing of the cane was a deliberate piece of entertainment, a thrilling spectacle, frightening even, the great swirling tongues of flame, the flashing, soaring rainbow-coloured sparks that spiralled into the sky, all designed to clear the giant grasses of snakes and strangling undergrowth.

What would she wear? In the two weeks since they had returned from the island she had come to appreciate that Leonora and her daughter, not to mention Marc who was almost as fashion-conscious, spent staggering sums of money on outfitting themselves for every conceivable occasion. All three were superbly turned out, though Rory had to concede not exactly to her taste, which was a little more conservative in Leonora's case and a great deal more so with regard to Tonia and Marc.

Still, tonight she had to do her father justice. They had, none of them, seen much of Brendan Sheridan or his partner, engaged as they were on a real estate development scheme which visualized clearing a great fringe of the rain forest. Development was being held up while a group of conservationists pleaded their case to which Rian, surprising all of them, had lent a sympathetic ear. Not so her father. It was Brendan Sheridan's intention to go right ahead with the scheme. People were willing to pay almost anything to have private retreats on the fringe of the rain forests; primeval, dense and mysterious with its coteries of orchids, every known fern, its fantastic bird life and the lovely allure of the unknown.

But for how long would it remain unknown? was the conservationist's argument. Australia was a big country with very few people in it, let them build their expensive retreats elsewhere. The rain forest was inviolate. And so it had gone on for weeks now. Soon the Government was expected to take a stand.

Rory walked towards the built-in wardrobe, mirror-fronted, almost a small room in itself. She looked along the rows of dresses. Nothing very spectacular there. And none too many of them either. Tonia, she knew, was wearing a very dashing pants suit, a glittery mesh of black and silver. She had nothing to top that and she had an inexplicable longing to do just that. No unfinished, unfledged *green girl*, but a soignée *femme du monde*. With her present wardrobe it should prove quite a test. Her hand bypassed an incredibly juvenile self-embroidered ivory organdie, a damask cotton, a silk jersey, the velvet hostess gown.

Until Kim had come into her life, she had very few opportunities for dining out, or going to parties, or indeed wearing evening clothes at all. Her hand hesitated over her one 'creation'. Her mother had chosen it for her to wear to Kim's annual bank dinner-dance. It was rather exquisite. Certainly her mother had possessed enviable good taste, if basically conservative – a sheer crêpe georgette, in deep honey beige with long deeply cuffed sleeves and a flowing skirt, a cascade of hand-made roses falling from the waist. The bodice was fitted with a high roll collar, no concession whatever to the alluring décolletage Tonia and Leonora often favoured. It was, however, very soft, very feminine, very elegant. Terribly conventional! she thought to herself, assailed by another vision of herself. Everything inside her screamed out for a swinging outfit, none of this demure old-world charm. But she hadn't much choice. Very carefully, for she was already made up with a little more drama than she normally effected, she stepped into the dress, adjusted the zipper with a few little manoeuvres, turned to face herself in the mirror.

She looked different. Quite different. Even her highly critical appraisal couldn't upset that verdict. The colour had always suited her, so it wasn't that. Perhaps it was her hair, falling in a deep natural wave about the creamy oval of her face. On the only other occasion she had worn the dress her mother had suggested the hairstyle; a soft Edwardian bun with soft little side tendrils. She had liked it well enough at the time. Now she had to admit that the total effect was quite different, but she still wasn't satisfied.

Her father would know. It was still early. She could catch him before he went downstairs.

She had reached the top of the staircase on her way to the other side of the house when Rian suddenly opened out the door of the large guest room he had practically made his own. He looked very striking, very elegant as only a tall man could be in evening clothes – conventionally black, which she had to admit she preferred to Marc's indigos and wildfire purples, but with a beautiful ruffled shirt, his cuff-links glittering under the light.

Despite any other inclinations, she could not deny herself the pleasure of letting her eyes play over him, the beautiful cut and cloth of his suit, the way it sat so impeccably on his wide shoulders. His eyes began to sparkle, a silvery glitter in his sardonic dark face.

'Tell me, is it in order for me to give *you* a critical

head-to-toe appraisal?'

'I'm sorry! Was I staring?' she asked unnecessarily, flushing a little, the colour clear under her luminous skin. 'I was just admiring your jacket. It's my father I want to see!'

'In that case, he's rather busy, my lamb. One or two phone calls to put through before he comes down for dinner.'

'Oh!' she stood there a little hesitant, while his eyes travelled over her with quick, masculine approval.

'Won't I do?' he asked suavely. 'And please don't spoil everything by looking scornful. It's something you do very well. Especially in the last week or so!'

She looked up at him, trying to fathom the dry note in his voice, then she sighed:

'Actually I only wanted to ask Father if this dress was all right!'

He looked at her through half closed lids, his dark arrogance making her eyes flash. 'My darling child, you don't expect me to believe that!'

'I'm afraid I *do*!' she said tightly, tilting her head almost defiantly.

He gave a brief laugh. 'Allow me to set your mind at rest. You look very presentable. It's the best I can manage under the circumstances. I wouldn't want to steal any of Marc's thunder. Just see he keeps you indoors!'

'But I don't want to look *presentable*!' she said scornfully, missing the sarcasm. 'I want to look . . .'

'. . . a tea rose. Exquisite, untouched, soft creamy petals faintly flushed, a beauty under glass?'

She felt her senses swimming a little weakly. It was ridiculous to think his voice had some special magic. She looked up at him trying to speak calmly, her eyes intense.

'Please, Rian, I just want to do Father justice. Tonia, I know . . .'

'You're *not* Tonia,' he cut her off, brutally emphatic. 'So don't try to be!'

A shimmering mist danced between him and the wall. There was something intoxicating in her quick rush of anger.

'At least not with *you*!'

He looked at her directly, his face hard, full of vitality and power, then his hand came down on her shoulder, jerking her towards him. 'Such resistance in so slender a shoulder!'

'You're hurting me!'

'I haven't *begun* to hurt you!'

With a shameful pang she realized her shoulder was curving to the palm of his hand. 'Do you think I don't know that?' she flashed at him. 'Do you think I don't know what kind of man you are?'

He drew an audible breath and his white teeth snapped. 'Now this is decidedly worth hearing. What kind of a man am I, my jewel-eyed little puritan, with your defective intuitions? What is it in you that wants to believe the worst of me?'

'What else is there to believe?'

His two hands closed over her shoulders and she fought against it, her limbs quivering, a great rose of desire unfurling in her like a devouring flower.

'What a little hypocrite you are!' he said softly, his strong hands on her.

Rory fell silent, averting her head, a pulse beating rapidly in her white throat, her emerald eyes dilated. She had never experienced anything like this before and she wanted to hit out at him for being the cause of it. His own eyes were hard and gleaming.

'Let's call a cease-fire! There's a time and a place for

everything!'

'May I go now?' she asked in a low voice.

'Why not?' His hands fell away from her. 'We agree upon some things. It's quite impossible for us to maintain a civilized relationship!'

'Impossible!' she agreed, not stopping to analyse her effect on him, her skirt swirling about her feet as she put safety and distance between them.

'You'll pay for that!' he said softer still, and her mouth trembled visibly. 'Go on!' he urged her, 'run like a child hiding away from a thunderstorm. But it won't be half far enough!'

Her eyes were green fire in the sudden pallor of her face. She believed him. Oh yes, she believed him. He was capable of anything.

'No!' she said recklessly, determined to show she was not to be intimidated, only to flee before the look in his eyes, conscious only of the rapid beating of her heart. There was no grace, no mercy, no letting up with McCallum!

Dinner was informal, buffet style, allowing their guests the opportunity to choose the dishes that appealed to them most. Tiny white scentless flowers, so as not to distract from the bouquet of the various wines, were arranged in squat silver goblets, with thin white lighted tapers between. The service was beautiful English bone china with a deeply etched gold encrustation, the silver lustrous with a sophisticated contemporary design, the tables covered in Irish linen and lace cloths, set in tandem, the one carrying a selection of wines, red and white, domestic and imported, the other laden with platters of prawn cutlets, lobster, rock oysters, Virginian baked ham, spring chicken with champignons, beef stroganoff, a variety of salads with dressings, and a *chilli con carne* with mounds of steaming, fluffy rice.

There were no more than twenty including the family and it seemed a sumptuous feast to Rory, who wasn't used to such affluence. Desserts and a cheese platter would follow to be served shortly before coffee and liqueurs. By nine-thirty everything was well under way. Two of the guests were an American milionaire and his wife, over for the big game fishing on the world's finest marlin grounds off the Barrier Reef. Rory listened in stunned silence to his pre-dinner conversation. It appeared he had spent well over thirty thousand dollars in the few weeks it took him to land the fish he wanted; a thousand-pound black marlin which, in any case, had to be towed out to sea the very next day and dumped. The other women of the party, with the exception of his wife, appeared to be equally staggered, but the menfolk, judging by their vivid faces, might have been visualizing the thrill of a lifetime.

Rory transferred her wide-eyed gaze to her father, laughing and relaxed, his arm thrown around Rian's shoulders, endeavouring to arrange a trip out while the big game season was right at its peak. Her first hostility towards this light-eyed tyrant increased, his maddening look of challenge and adventure. Whoever in their right mind would want to battle a thousand-pound monster of the deep, often for hours on end, only in most cases to lose the fish?

Leonora, in a beautiful burnished silk jersey, moved through the evening with slightly inhuman perfection, like some splendid vision, the success of the evening largely due to her efforts, a small masterpiece of organization. The food was superb, the wines equally so, the presentation mannered and gracious. No one monopolized the conversation. No one was excluded. The talk flowed over a wide range of subjects. Leonora saw to it, unobtrusively. Rory found herself watching her stepmother with deep admiration, puzzled to think that in so seemingly perfect a woman her father had failed to find happiness.

Seen together, in public at least, they were a columnist's dream of a handsome, well-to-do couple, supremely well adjusted. Nothing was ever as it seemed! Leonora's manner towards her husband was impeccable, her father's expressing a deep pride in so beautiful and capable a wife. What was really wrong? Why had they found no consolation in each other? Was marriage no more than a snare and a delusion? All the high hopes to come to nothing. It seemed such a pitiful waste. Rory moved back in her chair, her expression faintly melancholy, if anything, increasing her beauty.

Marc leaned towards her, speaking very softly, in his engaging barely accented voice. 'But you do not seem to like me, *piccola*, yet I have this irresistible desire to take your hand. You look so unhappy. You are not a very excellent actress, I think. If we were alone we could talk seriously for a few moments!' He looked hopefully into her face at that suggestion, then accepted his fate. 'One sometimes sees this sort of thing in children whose childhoods have been difficult.'

She smiled and turned to regard him with her strange eyes. 'I was really thinking how wonderful your mother is. What a superb hostess!'

'My mother is a rare woman. A very rare woman indeed!' Marc responded with touching seriousness. 'But what else is troubling you? You should be full of new hopes and dreams. After all, you have just met me. Instead there is a shadow in those very green eyes. It is not natural in one so young. I never, never myself allow anything to puzzle or disturb me. Life is for pleasure, a good time with no complications. Perhaps I shall make a bad end!'

Rory laughed involuntarily, while Marc, much heartened by that pretty sound, took off on a world of his own. Rory continued to smile at him. He amused her and his philosophy which she could never share, but he did have a number of endearing qualities and his happy, extrovert company turned her mood back to equanimity of a sort. If there were any shadows to be made, she made them herself.

Much later on the terrace there was dancing for those who cared to. Marc took her into his arms.

'Close as the beat of a heart!' he whispered near her ear.

A little while later she saw over Tonia's glossy head a hard, remote profile and she found herself frowning. In contrast, Tonia was as effervescent as a sparkling wine, animated, quick-moving, her body always in motion, her laugh pealing out like a blackbird, her liquid eyes endlessly pinned on a man's face. If the man was McCallum, so much the worse for her, Rory reasoned. Even Tonia, with all her obvious assets, had her work cut out to bring down such a lofty prize. She began to long for the evening to end, her efforts to appear normal were draining all her resources. Marc, at least, had no objection to a little seeming mystery and reserve in a woman; nuzzling her ear, becoming more outrageous by the minute, yet she took no more notice of him than if he were, indeed, her brother. There was no explaining physical attraction. A man moved in a certain way. . . .

What was the matter with her? All was not well, but beyond that she refused to pry, thrusting realities away with furtive fingers. Marc's gaiety and admiration bore her along like a spring tide and she felt gratitude towards him which he obviously did not interpret as such – and how could he with her mouth softening, a dreamy, yearning expression in her eyes?

Only once during the evening did she catch a pair of light-grey eyes and all at once he was not smiling, not the urban sophisticate, looking back at her with inexorable resolve, almost as though she were his enemy. She looked away from that odd little twist near his mouth, but not before she saw Leonora claim him with shining simplicity a fine veil of colour washing her face making her look younger, softer, more vulnerable. Something was there under that seeming candour, the smooth façade, Rory was sure of it. But *what*? Leonora, in her mid-forties, was still a very beautiful woman. Perhaps she was lonely. Bored? She was not entirely happy in her marriage. It was a dangerous state of affairs. Moreover, Leonora bore the legacy of a Latin temperament, for all her regal calm. A woman, and a life-long beauty, would need to know herself desirable. Anything less would be unthinkable, scarcely able to be borne. A woman was no less, but more so a woman when she was forty.

A thousand jangled little thoughts spun round in Rory's mind. She liked Leonora and admired her; she could well understand her longing for complete fulfilment. Why didn't her father love his wife? Surely she was everything a man could want in a woman? He had said he had loved his first wife, Sara, at least for a time when they were young. Yet Rory's memories of her mother were, for the most part, unhappy ones. It was all so wildly illogical. Sara Sheridan had left her mark on her husband as well as her daughter, a feeling of guilt and self-recriminations for having, in their respective ways, failed her. Perhaps happiness was not built on such beginnings as these?

With a little shock she realized Marc was holding her hand 'as a brother might!' and she smiled at him and tried to fix her mind on him, the mobile laughing face full of suppressed excitement. She made a tremendous effort to come alive and responded very charmingly when Leonora called them both over to her group, graciously including her in the family unit. That her father loved her, and wished to 'show her off', was balm to her aching young heart. And it was aching! There was no point at all in trying to analyse her extraordinary reactions to the evening, she had to concentrate on getting through it. Yet her father's guests found her beauty, her look of breeding, her delicate fastidiousness wholly charming.

When, at last, it was all over, she changed out of her clothes and came downstairs again to lend a hand in restoring things to order. She was puzzled and perturbed by her own attitudes almost like a personality change, but then a woman's moods were apt to be sudden and remarkably complete. There was surprisingly little to do and Maria didn't take kindly to her kitchen being invaded, however well-meant the gesture. Belguardo might one day well be hers, but while Maria was about, the kitchen, *never*!

Somewhere in the house, Tonia was singing gaily. Leonora had kissed her cheek and bade her good night. Now it was all over, she had come wide awake. Someone was moving out on the terrace. She saw a momentary flash of a pale shirt. Marc had been in the living-room a short time before. Perhaps he had gone out to smoke a cigarette, for despite all the cautions and warnings, he saw them as an extension to himself.

Rory moved out into the pale radiance of moonlight, the long golden beams falling from the house. She caught a faint movement and walked towards it, her voice warm and friendly, with a faint lilt.

'Well, Maria has just tossed me out of the kitchen. I

thought I'd join you in a breath of air!'

The shadow moved and straightened. Much too tall for Marc. Too rangy. 'Oh!' she said inadequately, 'I thought it was Marc!'

'That goes without saying! I did register the tone of voice – simple, uncomplicated. I've never heard it!'

She was half in, half out of the shadows, a lake of light over her face and the pale lemon of her shirt. Her slender body was poised warily, seemingly on the verge of flight.

'I'm going down to check the fires.' He spoke abruptly in a take-it-or-leave-it voice. 'They'll be watched throughout the night. Do you want to come? Of course, there's always the chance I'm acting out of an admirable if wrongly channelled sense of friendliness!'

She stood staring at him, suspended in a strange void, an involuntary tightening of excitement in her throat. It would always be there, that excitement.

'There must be some simple and infallible method of getting on with you,' she said in a low-pitched voice. 'Tonia . . . Leonora . . . seem to have achieved it!'

'You haven't struck it yet?'

'No!'

'Are you coming or not?' he asked very crisply indeed.

She longed to be able to say no, but she was beaten down by various little hammers. The way the light caught the side of his dark face, the icy sheen of his eyes, the gleam of high cheekbones, the deeply shadowed cleft of his chin. He too had changed his clothes. His shirt glimmered palely, opened carelessly at the throat, exposing the teak tan column of his throat.

'Well, I've exhausted my supply of overtures!' he said grimly, and turned on his heel, disappearing into the night-time jungle of the garden. Rory flew after him, released from her spell, a little breathless, as she caught at his arm.

'Oh, please, Rian! It can't have escaped you that you do your level best to antagonize me!'

'Perhaps – just a little!' His hard expression relented a little and he slowed down his long paces to match her own. 'And now with such an excellent opportunity! I've been looking forward to it all evening.'

She glanced at him quickly, with a kind of devastated amazement. 'They say a woman can grow used to anything!'

'A comfort certainly, but not necessarily a desirable state of affairs. Let me say at the outset, with a girl like you I prefer to use shock tactics.'

She looked back at the dark face briefly turned to her and its exact expression brought her to a shaking stop. He laughed under his breath, his grip on her elbow one of steely courtesy.

'You're definitely not running away! Stay and face the consequences. Everything falls flat without a little daring!'

Angry words rushed to her lips, but she could say nothing at all; a strange magnetism was working between them. He looked at her intently. A full moon was riding high, illuminating the driveway. A green fire blazed from her pale face, her hair a little disordered by the wind, a thick swirling mane about her face, brushing her cheeks.

'Why do you hate me?' he asked pleasantly.

Hate you! *Hate you!* her heart drummed outside of her body.

'It's pretty difficult not to,' she responded equally pleasantly. 'Tell me, did you enjoy this evening?'

'Did you?'

She turned her head away, a shadow in her eyes. The

118

temptation to unburden herself was almost irresistible. He was hard and unyielding, but he understood her and they both knew it. A night bird thrilled in the trees startling her a little. Her voice had a soft little catch to it:

'They seemed so happy this evening. My father . . . Leonora.'

'What were you expecting?' His voice had the thread of steel. Every instinct warned her to be careful.

'Please, Rian!' she was almost pleading with him. 'Don't treat me like a child. You know what I mean.'

'The way you're going, you're going to make yourself thoroughly miserable. Assuming the attitudes of a loving wife doesn't mean a woman will turn into a happy loving wife, but it does take a good deal of strain off the situation. A by-product, if you like. Don't brood about it. It's not really my affair, nor yours!'

'I can't help it!'

'I thought as much. The usual feminine lack of acceptance of the status quo!'

They seemed to be moving in a dream like slow motion towards the front line of cane. The towering conflagration that had drowned out the light of the moon had died a little, the fires were well under control, shooting sparks like fireworks over the main body of the flames.

'There it is,' Rian said laconically. 'An arsonist's dream or a firefighter's nightmare!'

'It's exciting, isn't it? A little barbaric!' Her teeth gleamed in her parted mouth. She moistened her top lip with the tip of her tongue.

'Rian?'

'Yes?' He looked down at her briefly, the tension still there.

'Why is Leonora so unhappy? And she is, isn't she?

Under that splendid passivity. She seems to turn to you . . .!'

'Drop it, honey, while you're in front!'

'But I'm not going to!' she said, breathing fast, 'though it's clever of you to suggest it! I want to force your hand. I had some proof this evening. . . .'

'Go on!' he taunted her, his voice hard, abrupt, rather terrifying. 'The more I see of you, the more convinced I am that your mind is a seething little labyrinth of obscurities! Don't tell me you're frightened at last? Not you with your red hair and green eyes!'

'I'm frightened of nothing!' she said, her face paling, but a light of resolution in her eyes.

'Good, because you're going to need all the courage you've got!'

He turned on her with the taut alertness of a hunter. The flames threw his head into relief, an aura about his dark head and shoulders.

'*No!*' Passionate repudiation was in her voice, quivering in the air.

He came on as if he had never heard her, his own emotions too fierce. Her eyelids flickered and fell as he moved towards her, his height exaggerated in the glare of the flames. She was seized by a great agitation, a leap of primitive fear, like the breathless second before lightning struck. He was fully aroused, and what did she really know of him?

He pulled her into his arms and bent his head, kissing her with a kind of elemental hunger, an underlying sex antagonism, not satiated by the feel of her soft, parted mouth, his hand threading through her hair, twisting her head back into the curve of his shoulder so that she couldn't escape him, kissing her over and over again. She was wreathed in flames, a consuming fire, the violence of emotions she had not known she possessed. Her head was humming and aching, her mouth under his the vortex of fiery sparks.

When finally he released her she was trembling so convulsively he had to hold her to prevent her from falling. His dark face was a carving. He had control of himself. She was forced to acknowledge it, appalled by the complete disintegration of all her long-held defences, all sense of restraint.

'Leave me!' she said in a voice of splintering glass, her eyes revealing her tormented state, her limbs overcome by long, slow rigours.

He gave a low laugh that bore no relationship to amusement of any kind, his eyes so coldly brilliant they almost seared her on contact. 'If I took my hands from you you'd fall down, you little coward. It's the only reason I'm holding you now. I hope we've both learnt a lesson from that fierce little encounter, necessary though it seems to have been!'

Rory couldn't look into his face, her burning flesh imprinted with the memory of her passionate yielding. She wanted nothing more than to be able to hit him and run, hurt him as he was hurting her – deliberately, for he was cruel, but her limbs refused to obey her. She was utterly devastated. It didn't seem possible to *hate*, yet yearn to be made love to, at the same time.

He turned her away, his arm hard and compelling at her back. The moonlight etched the poignant outline of her face. It looked very young and defenceless. Nearing the house she made an instinctive movement of withdrawal, but his hand locked about her wrist. He was as hard as honed steel and as ruthless and he had pierced her every defence. She was safe no longer. Safe within the citadel she had built herself. Deftly he had stripped it away from her!

CHAPTER SEVEN

FROM the moment he stepped off the plane, Kim was a stranger. And this was the man she contemplated marrying? He was a little pale after the long flight – or she was used to deeply tanned faces – his blond head gleaming, suit, shirt, tie, immaculate, yet he looked out of place in such a colourful casual atmosphere. It simply wasn't fair of her to feel this rush of disappointment. What had she expected? To go weak at the knees? Kim had never had that effect on her.

Rory waited for him to walk through the gates from the tarmac, feeling the smile on her face, forced and insincere, and she was bitterly ashamed of it. This was Kim who had offered such comfort to her. She turned up her mouth and he touched it coolly, a public demonstration of affection acceptable to both of them, but his hands on hers were hard.

'It's been far too long, darling! And those letters! A mine of information if you're interested in sugar cane, and I'm *not!*'

He smiled at her sidelong and they turned and walked into the sudden cool of the terminal building. Kim eased his collar around his neck. 'God, it's hot up here! Don't they ever get a winter?'

'We don't get much of a one ourselves!'

'True! Only remarking, darling!' He opened his eyes at her and she had to smile.

He felt a quick upthrust of desire. Life in the sun suited her; her skin was veiled with the lightest sheen of apricot, her hair swinging free as he liked it, shining in the warm, sun-laden air, narrow flared trousers over long, slender legs, a heavily fringed suede jacket over a white silk blouse. She looked different. Very poised, up-dated, and she turned a lot of heads as they always seemed to turn for a good-looking redhead.

Rory returned his smile, a mask for reality; her familiar Kim was no more than a nice-looking stranger. Surely this odd, fey feeling would wear off. Out in the car park it still hadn't. Kim loaded his cases into the boot and turned to face her, his mood one of elation.

'Want me to drive? Nice little bus. Not yours, surely? I won't believe it!' But he looked very much as if he wanted to.

'Tonia's,' she supplied a little dryly, looking along the perfect profile of the Volvo coupé. 'She was kind enough to let me have a loan of it.'

'And if you bust it up plenty more where that came from, eh? *Tonia?* She'd be the stepsister?'

'Yes.'

'What's she like?' Kim held the door for her and she slipped into the passenger seat, without protest and only the faintest niggle of irritation. He was, after all, the better driver.

'Very pretty!' she answered easily. 'Very vivacious. You'll like her. In fact, she's altogether more your type!'

'Don't you believe it!' he said huskily, his eyes slipping over her mouth. In another minute he was in the driver's seat, switching on the ignition. 'And the others?' he prompted, his eyes slipping over the dash with pleasure.

'You'll like them too. Leonora, my stepmother, is the most beautiful woman I've ever seen or am ever likely to see!'

'Italian, you mean,' Kim commented with a faint smile.

'I'm not altogether with you!' she said after a short silence. 'Italian certainly, like one of the beautiful women of antiquity or a classic carving, enormously enigmatical!'

Her voice was so sincere, Kim took another look at her. 'Well, that's all very well, dear, but I'll have good old British stock every time. One can't outgrow the old tribal traditions!' His eyes sharpened over her. 'Tell me, who's this McCallum character? You've only mentioned him once or twice, but he sounds like a big wheel. Would I have to have his O.K. for a job?'

'Very likely.' Rory's tone was non-committal. 'He's Father's partner and he has a great deal of say. Father relies on him implicitly and as well he's very fond of him. I imagine Rian is the sort of son he might have had!'

'Now that's interesting!' Kim said wryly. '*Rian?* You have progressed, my dear. Last time I heard of him, it was Mr. McCallum and a dour, doughty Scot. How old?'

'About thirty-five or six, but his manner makes age group unimportant. He's very imperious, but it's quite natural, I'm forced to concede. I suppose when you're forceful and clever you accept it like I accept having red hair. At least it's the best excuse I can find for him!'

'Don't like him, eh, sweetie?' Kim asked complacently. 'I can hear just the faintest trace of bitchiness!'

'No, I don't like him!' Kim said emphatically. 'He's not that kind of man. There's something elemental about him. At any rate, he arouses powerful instincts!'

'*Oh!*' Kim drawled the single word instantly, dropping McCallum as if he couldn't bear to hear any name but his own. 'And your father?'

'He's not as I often imagined him, but he's everything I want him to be. We're very close.'

'And that's how it should be! Let's face it, darling, your mother was wrong all along!'

She winced a little. 'Let's not talk about that. I still miss my mother, you know. You might see where people are going wrong, but it still doesn't prevent your loving them. It's not easy to make the right decisions when one is handicapped with a difficult nature. Sometimes the demands of one's nature are cruelly destructive, changing and undermining the course of a life. Mother might have found happiness with a different kind of man – certainly not Father. I can see that quite well. But they married very young and one outgrew the other.'

Kim nodded his fair head a little impatiently as though all that had very little to do with him. 'Speaking of marriage, when are we going to set the date? I know you're the only girl in the world for me, darling. It's been forced home on me since you've been away!'

She couldn't help the little instinctive thrill of dismay.

'Don't let's rush anything, Kim!'

He didn't answer but pulled the car off the road, his profile rather grim. He switched off the ignition and turned to face her, his arm slipping along the back of the seat. 'See here, Rory, if you loved me you wouldn't use that tone of voice, neither would you dither. Don't tell me you've changed your mind. I thought you had too much integrity for that!'

'I've hurt you!' she said inadequately, seeing it was so, not wishing to spoil all his bright pleasure on arrival.

'Since when did you mind hurting me?' he asked with a faintly bitter smile. 'You're a cruel little cat, and the wonder of it is, you don't even know!'

Her eyes were troubled, as green as a leaf in the shade. 'But we're not even engaged yet, Kim!'

'Well, let's get engaged, if that's what you want. I don't want to rush you, but I can't see the point of hanging about. I do know this – your mother did a lot of harm over the years. It's a wonder you can see straight at all, but you're basically warm-blooded. Anyone else would be an out-and-out man-hater, a riproaring old maid, frigid as the Antarctic!' He took her hands tightly and kissed them. 'See here, darling, I'll work for you and make you happy, I swear it, but you have to open out. I've only had one little peck at the airport. Kiss me, Rory. Properly this time!' His hand slipped under her thick hair, caressing her nape, then he kissed her, gently at first but with rising passion. She tried to respond, letting him part her mouth, her own moving. 'Promise to marry me now!' he whispered against her mouth.

She was silent and he released her a little angrily. 'What's with you anyway, darling? I'm not trying to lock you into a situation!'

She straightened in her seat again. 'Perhaps you are!'

He looked at her intensely. In the segment of sunlight her skin had all the pinks and golds of copper, her lashes thickly tangled, her eyes brilliant within the dark red mane of her hair.

'You're beautiful!' he said ardently and with a faint shade of bitterness. 'It's just as well, I suppose, you *are* the way you are, otherwise I'd spend the rest of my days in a torment of jealousy!'

'And you think there would never be any need for it?' She swept her hands over her hair with a queer restlessness.

'No, I *don't*!' Kim said, very sure of her. 'And I'm glad of it. You inspire hunger and urgency in a man, yet you have none yourself!'

Oh, God, what nonsense, she thought to herself with a dart of pain and remembrance that changed her expression. She could never concede that! Not now, not in one million years or the life span of a star.

Kim's blond hair rose in a crest and he looked as if he was being threatened. 'Look here, darling, I know your mother and father were miserably unhappy together. I know your mother fretted herself into an early grave. I know she took it out on you and hammered all her old hates home, but that's in the past. There are disillusioned people in all walks of life, but marriage is still the best answer for most of us.'

'Providing it's a selfless love we have for one another!' she said with quick foresight, 'and often not even then!' Her glowing head dropped into her hands. 'Oh, I don't really know what I'm talking about. Can't we leave it for a while, please, Kim? You've only just arrived!'

He leaned forward and switched on the ignition, put the car in gear and drew back on to the road. 'All right, we'll leave it. But not for long. Life is pretty tame without you. One thing we won't have to worry about is money, the hellish, never-ending budgeting and saving and scraping along. Demoralizing!'

'Why won't we?' she asked in amazement.

'Come off it, sweetie!' He flickered a smile at her, his eyes dancing, white teeth gleaming. 'Your father is a millionaire!'

'My *father* is a millionaire!' she said tersely, 'but I'm not! I'd like to work to attain my goals. I don't want the man I marry taking money off my father. I doubt whether he'd contribute in any case. He made *his* own way. Marrying me is no insurance for the future, let me tell you!'

'You have told me, darling!' He drew a deep breath,

his teeth snapping with resentment. 'Please don't fly off at a tangent and don't say things you don't mean. I'm trying to be realistic. You might! Verbal communication *is* important. Why should we evade the truth? I've got three weeks' leave. In that time I intend to line up a few things. The first one is you – the most important of all. You're beautiful and I love you. A bit cold, perhaps, but we can soon change that. In fact you're changing already, if that kiss was anything to go on. Next, I intend to approach your father about a job. Don't worry, I'm no slacker. Anyone in the bank can tell you that. In fact they have told you. I'll give as good as I get and I'm as ambitious as the next man. It's in the natural order of things for your father to want the best for you, his only child. I can't see him letting you struggle. If he can make things easier for you, he will. After all, he's supported you all along. Try to be a little realistic, darling, if it's not too much to ask. All this high-flown working for goals and all the rest of it! Work by all means, but collect all the perks at the same time!'

Rory was cautious now and he sensed her withdrawal.

'How can I expect you to understand me when I can't understand myself?' she said quietly.

'But I *do* understand you, darling! I know you've more than the normal need for privacy. In fact, you're a bit too much on the reserved side!'

She pushed back her hair, her voice very dry. 'Thank you, Kim! Your opinion is of great value to me!'

Surprisingly he took it at face value. 'Now don't worry, darling, together we'll get over your little hang-ups. You'll see! We've just got to be honest with each other. It's essential for a workable relationship. You're like all women, you crave security.'

Her face was quite unreadable. 'It all depends what

security you mean. I've always had financial security. There are other kinds!'

'But none so important, darling. Believe me! You've always been one of this world's lilies and you don't really know it. Priceless, that, but it's a great part of your charm. Look at your hands – exquisite. You've never done a decent day's work in your life!'

'That doesn't mean I can't!' she said without heat, realizing with an incongruous sense of shock that Kim lacked the capacity to make her angry. 'Or that I wouldn't want to. No one as yet has required it of me, that's all. I don't think you really know what I want at all, Kim!'

He clicked his teeth in outright annoyance. 'Well, this is getting us nowhere. A first-class quarrel and we've only been together, what? Twenty minutes? One might be forgiven for thinking we didn't need to get married at all! The thing is, Rory, and you'll have to face it, you're frightened of giving yourself. Frightened of giving too much. That is your mother's legacy. It will take time to get rid of it. One of these days you're going to trust me to know what's best for you!' His eyes slipped over her profile and his voice softened. 'I love you, I want you, I need you. It's as simple as that. All I require is for you to return those sentiments. I was under the impression you did!'

He was visibly thrown off balance by her attitude, she could see that. She leaned across and touched his hand.

'I'll try, Kim. I'll try!' But it would seem to be a very tall order indeed. Perhaps Kim was right and there was something wrong with her. She only knew she viewed the prospect of walking into the future with Kim Barrett as ultimately impossible. The difficulty would be in telling him. How could he accept or understand it when she had clung to him while her mother had been alive? Now she didn't need him at all. What had changed all that? But she knew. Yes, she knew! Kim was right – she wasn't honest. Not with him. Not with herself. She could only struggle against her menaced peace of mind. With Kim at least she would be treated as a peer, but with another man . . . what man? . . . with *him*, she knew, she would inevitably be dominated.

Kim turned to her with a wry smile. 'Oh, why did I have to fall in love? Why couldn't I have been happy with my stamp collection!'

From the start it was Tonia who stagemanaged Kim's visit, so that to an outsider it might have seemed that Tonia was the object of his desire and Rory the one who had inadvertently brought them together. In male company, Tonia sparkled, her quick restlessness and mercurial charm never more in evidence. Her liking for Kim had been immediate and mutual to the point where Kim informed Rory in strictest confidence, and not without kindness that she might do well to emulate her stepsister's vivacity and lightness of heart.

Rory had smiled, a little ironically, and said nothing. The heart of the matter was, and she could see it plainly enough now, though her physical image continued to transfix Kim's mind, he was far more in tempo with a bright, talkative girl, and it didn't matter about what! Such a girl, frivolous perhaps but merry, drew him out and made him shine within his set limits. Tonia did this quite simply and well. So all four of them, Rory and Kim, Tonia and Marc, went about everywhere together; parties and picnics, swimming and boating and motoring, a trek through the fringe of the rain forest, which wasn't a great success owing to Tonia's basic dislike of self-ambulation, and before Kim was to return to the capital, a proposed trip to Sorella, probably by the inter-island flying boat.

Only occasionally did Kim chafe under these arrangements, and then not so much because of Tonia's presence, but rather Marc's dark-eyed exuberance, his open admiration which was the breath of life to him, for Rory and the 'flowery compliments that fell from his lips wholesale. Marc, for his part, took a kind of malicious, snickering satisfaction in Kim's stolidly concealed displeasure, for fear of offending the family, but Marc knew with intuitive accuracy that Rory's affections were scarcely engaged. No one mentioned the engagement, but it was a burning question in the minds of all of them.

That night they were off, the four of them, to the monthly dinner dance at the Country Club. Rory went downstairs a little early to catch a few moments alone with her father. Brendan Sheridan had proved a genial if somewhat absentee host, but Rory had the clear notion that he had no great opinion of Kim, one way or the other. Neither was he alone in that, his opinion clearly reflected in that of his partner, or so it seemed to Rory, who chafed a little under such urbane, civilized indifference even if Kim, the object of it, appeared not to notice. In fact he didn't, visibly impressed by both men, finding their way and his poles apart, but all that could be rectified once he was part of the family.

She moved under the brilliant light from the chandelier and on to the study. It was Rory's constant worry now that her father drove himself too hard, for on the odd day he could look deathly tired working the long, irregular hours of big business. He seemed to be forever professionally engrossed, never more than a few feet from the telephone, the great point of contact, pouring bursts of brusque dialogue into the mouthpiece. For the most part he was either ringing Cal, meeting Cal, greeting Cal, or sending Cal interstate to deputize for him at some meeting or other. One thing was certain, he trusted his partner implicitly, but to Rory the world of high finance could be extremely oppressive; coups and counter-coups, the pushing ahead of one's arguments and plans against all opposition. It was a ruthless, cutthroat business, and yet with a mingled pride and dismay Rory realized that men like her father and Rian seemed to thrive on it, thoroughly attuned to its demands.

She hesitated a moment outside the study door, conscious that she was looking her best and pleased to be able to show herself off to her father in her evening finery. Apart from that she felt no great joy in her appearance. Good or bad, without Rian, everything fell flat. She hadn't seen him for the best part of a week, but it was strange how he haunted her mind.

Her father called to her and she opened the door, putting her head around first, the heavy sweep of her hair a living aura around her face. Her father was hunched over the telephone covering the mouthpiece with one hand, but he noted with one part of his mind the new sea-green chiffon, the gauzy green mother-of-pearl roses and glittery leaves that encrusted the low oval neckline and the tiny, set-in sleeves. He smiled and made a little gesture of approval, beckoning her in, and Rory made a swift turn in the centre of the room to display to best effect the long beautiful skirt that swirled about her feet like sea foam. He watched her a while, then his smiling face sobered abruptly as he removed his hand to say violently into the phone:

'The hell I did! Look here, Baxter, don't try to put that one across me. No, I'm not being too quick off the mark. Cal told you ... right-oh, that suits me too. Better get your girl to make an appointment. Good.

Good. Got you!' He braced his broad shoulders and slammed the phone down. As abruptly as he had turned it on, his expression cleared miraculously and he was smiling again so that Rory hád the curious impression that he lived on two levels at once.

He flashed her a quick, comprehending smile, noting her faint bewilderment and the cause of it.

'You're just what I need, Rory girl – a period of blessed respite. Some ventures give more trouble than others. For the first time in years my wisdom seems to be in question!'

'The rain forest?' she asked with quick perception.

'Right in one. Even Cal is not entirely in tune with me.' He shoved back his black leather swivel chair and linked his hands behind his silver leonine head. 'He's a complex character, our Cal. Terribly shrewd and hard-headed, inclined to be a bit impatient. Action, not arguments, with Cal. Always the logical conclusion and in the shortest possible time, but he has this great love for his natural environment. It's hampering me a bit. We're always so closely in step. I don't like to go against him!'

'But he's with you, isn't he, Father?' she asked quickly.

'Oh yes, he's with me, but his heart's not really in it. Cal's one of those men who think generations ahead. He wants his son to be able to see the rain forest for himself, not hear about how it used to be. His boyhood was spent in the wilds exploring it with his father. That's how I got to know him. His father was a great pal of mine, but no business man, not in any sense. He was a born adventurer. His wife died early on and he brought up Cal in the most haphazard fashion. After I came to know them a while I had to take a hand. Cal had too much potential; even as a boy he was quite remarkable. His father once owned the land Belguardo stands on – did you know that?'

'No, I didn't. Rian never mentioned it!'

'He wouldn't!' her father grunted, and suddenly laughed at some passing thought. 'Anyway the one reason Cal is with me is, if we don't undertake this development scheme somebody else *will*, as soon as they can rake up the capital. At least Cal seems to think we can handle it the right way. After all, it will be pretty pricey territory and people who can afford that kind of thing and love their privacy aren't going to destroy the natural beauty of their surroundings, rather enhance it – or so I'd like to think. The whole project will be scrupulously overseen. Architectural designs, plans submitted for approval, that sort of thing. People know me, my name, they know they can expect the best. And the Government haven't come down on top of us as I had a few qualms they might. You see, Rory girl, it all goes under the name of progress. Some of us fight it, and hang out as long as we can, but we have to face realities, change is inevitable. There are few virgin strongholds left in the world. We won't violate the rain forest, I can promise you that. But enough of my troubles. You look beautiful, darling, like a glossy ad . . . Sweet Spring . . . or something like that. You can't be making it easy for young Barrett. Where are you off to tonight?'

Rory started to wander about, evading those cool, clever eyes:

'The Country Club – the usual sort of thing. Tonia and Marc are coming along!'

'God!' Her father exploded into laughter. 'In my day I'd never have stood for it. It was a *pas de deux* every time! And Tonia and Marc! They're so damned noisy! What makes young people so noisy, can you tell me? Ah well, I'd better keep my mind flexible, they're engaging young pups if it comes to that, but they'll have to grow up soon. Marc at any rate, he thinks life is just one long giggle from start to finish, but a little struggle is necessary for character building. What he does about the plantation isn't up to much, and then Cal handles all the financial side of it and he can ill afford the time!'

Rory passed by the desk and her father caught her hand, holding her still. 'What are you going to do about Barrett?'

'Father!' She looked down at him, her eyes brooding, enormous, faintly melancholy.

'Don't hedge, darling. A blind man wearing sunglasses could tell you don't love him or anything like it!'

'Is it so obvious?' she asked, low-voiced. A closeness seemed to flow between them that settled her mind. 'I don't, I'm afraid.'

'Well, if you don't, you don't!' her father said in his calm emphatic way, 'and I must say I'm glad to hear it. Not for selfish reasons – I want a grandson perhaps more than the next man – but I must be sure you have the right man, the man to understand you and make you happy, or as close as we get in this world. Young Barrett clearly will not. A pleasant enough young chap, but lightweight, essentially mediocre!'

She smiled a shade wryly at that devastating pronouncement.

'That's a little cruel, isn't it, Father?'

'I suppose it is, darling, as the truth often is!' he agreed equably. 'Now do you want me to give him a job, or what? He's got an eye to the main chance, you know. In fact if he wasn't so obviously and genuinely smitten with you I'd kick him out!'

She laughed a little at his ruthlessness. 'I don't see why you have to give him a job!'

'Well then, when are you going to tell him and get it over with? There's no point in letting him build up false hopes. It's not fair to either of you. Of course he's getting a damn good holiday, and strangely enough I don't think you'll break his heart, my darling. It's the physical you he's attracted to, and that kind of emotion can be fierce but shallow. Let him look somewhere else. He'll find comfort soon enough. Take my word for it!'

'Well, that would be a blessing!' Rory said lightly, her anxiety concealed under a bright mask. 'Every morning I get up with the intention of telling him and every night I go to bed . . . mission unaccomplished! I rather shirk hurting him. He was very kind to me when Mother was alive.'

'Kind?' Her father stared at her in astonishment. 'Surely to God you weren't contemplating marrying him because he was *kind*? I've known women, good women too, give a man hell because he was kind to them – too kind. I don't know quite what it is with women, but some of them like to be hurt. Some of them can't bear the slightest discordant note. It causes them pain. Whatever conclusions I've reached about women they've always been proved wrong – one reason why I turned to the relatively uncomplicated field of big business!'

Rory shivered as if an icy draught had blown through the room. 'But why should I have overestimated my feelings for him, Father? Am I so immature?'

'Let's say, my darling, Kim Barrett was well within the limits of your experience. Sara would never have encouraged you to lead a full, varied life. She counted safety above all else, and to love a man, really love him, is a confession of dependence in a woman, complete and absolute – a total surrender, no matter what anyone says. It's simple biology, much as a lot of women fight it.

But I don't think you're like that, Rory. I think you could stand a passionate attachment. Think about it, my darling! Is it safety you want? Are you incapable of learning? Incapable of change? Content to be ignorant of the world you live in? No, I don't think so. Not at all, despite the way Sara brought you up with all its painful stresses. You're going to make a fine woman, not shirking life.'

'I know I love you, Father,' she said softly, her eyes iridescent.

'Well, that's the very devil, sweetheart, because I feel the same way about you myself!'

Tenderness flowed over her in waves, the infinite contentment of knowing herself home, a beam of golden light in the long night. She bent and kissed her father's cheek with all the ache of the lost years in the gesture. He covered her hand and patted it, at the same moment his attention distracted by a loud rap on the door. There was an instant's pause, then the door opened. Rian stood in the open doorway, the glitter of the big chandelier behind his head, tall, very dark and vivid with the appearance of a man in a hurry. The collar of his jacket was still upturned against the night breeze, giving him a faintly rakish appearance, his eyes a startling shock in so dark a face. His mouth was smiling, but the light eyes were cool and watchful.

'I don't think you two realize what a very good-looking pair you are!' He walked into the room and shut the door behind him. 'How are you, Bren? Rory?'

Brendan Sheridan got up from his chair with an exclamation of surprise and pleasure, his hand outthrust to the younger man.

'God damn it, Cal, I didn't expect you back until tomorrow at least. Don't tell me you've wrung a decision out of them already?'

'A big yes to that one, with "wrung" the operative word, but we can talk about that later. Right now I could do with something to eat. The plane only touched down an hour ago and I came straight on to the house. It's been a long day!'

Brendan Sheridan gave his partner a quick, thoughtful look not unmixed with speculation. 'Why, certainly, Cal. Leonora's out – some Arts Council meeting or other. And the children are going on to a dinner dance.'

'I can see that!' The silvery glance licked over the silent girl. 'That's a ravishingly pretty dress, Rory. I could use you for the *Saraband* and rename it *Sea Sprite*!'

Brendan Sheridan smiled at his daughter. 'Look after Cal, sweetheart, while I go see Maria.'

'I'll go, Father,' she volunteered quickly – too quickly, for that shapely mouth turned down with derision.

Her father missed it, continuing to smile. 'No, don't bother, darling, I'll see to it. What would you like, Cal?'

'Anything at all,' he said lightly, noting Rory's dilemma with interest. 'Tell Maria not to go to any bother. Just make it substantial!'

'Something substantial coming up! Come to that, I think I'll join you. I've had precious little myself and what with your good news you've made my appetite pick up. I'll go fetch us a bottle of something special from the cellar. Just the stimulant we need!' He walked off with an airy gesture that included the two of them, his step light, his eyes gleaming.

Left alone, a dark glitter of tension webbed its way across the room linking the two of them. Rory looked away from the dark profile, afraid of giving away too much, too soon. She felt shaky with excitement just having him back again. Rian McCallum was a thorn in her soft flesh, never dismissed, never forgotten. She looked, had she known it, very young, very fragile, very endangered. The faint look of strain on her face made it almost ethereal, the oblique light emphasized her elegant bone structure. Unwillingly her eyes were lured back to him, his head against the light in blinding focus.

'Don't look at me like that, little one,' he said dryly. 'I'm not about to break all ten commandments at once!'

'I'm sure you're not, Rian, though your life history would make fascinating reading!'

'I assure you, my child, I couldn't spin it out to more than one volume. But there's always the chance of fresh material!' His glance flickered over her and she stood passive and immobile, feeling his gaze like a powerful electric current, exciting and rather fearsome.

'So you're going out?' he said lightly. 'Your mood doesn't appear to be one of radiant pleasure. Tell me, when is the engagement party? I hurried back with that in mind!'

She caught her breath at his bold insolence, the flash of devilry that was never very far from his eyes.

'You don't change, do you, Rian?'

'What is it you want or expect?'

Her skin prickled and her spine tautened defensively. 'I don't know,' she said truthfully, 'but I'm sure I'd never get it from you!'

His glance struck her and held it. 'It's the very devil, isn't it, little one, this unsatisfied curiosity! It feeds on itself. Perhaps if I knew more about *you*, I wouldn't spend so much time wondering just what makes that timid little heart of yours tick over!' He turned away from her with one of his lightning gestures, taking a cigarette from the box on the table, lighting it, speaking over his shoulder. 'Where are you off to tonight?'

'The Country Club,' she found herself saying a little dazedly. 'Marc and Tonia are coming.'

'I envy you the experience!' he said suavely. 'Imagine *two* young hotheads glowering across the table at one another! At very least, there's safety in numbers, and that's what you want, isn't it, Rory? Safety. The familiar and the safe. And who knows, you might have got it if you hadn't come up to Belguardo!'

His dark, high-cheekboned face was intent upon her, about him an aura of coiled strength, a hair-trigger alertness she had to defend herself from.

'You like hurting me, don't you, Rian?'

'*Am I* hurting you?'

'You know damned well you are!'

He shrugged his wide shoulders, his eyes veiled by smoke. 'I find it difficult not to, though sometimes I have to submit to the light of common sense!'

As always when she looked at him, Rory felt the same old desperation, the tormented desire to have things different between them. Her slender hands were clasped tight, a glittery leaf on her dress casting a triangle of light on to her cheekbone. 'Somehow I thought, or rather *hoped*, we might be friends. It was a mistake I have to admit to. Total defeat!'

His voice was hard, full of irony. 'Don't tell me you're ignorant of the reasons?' He straightened abruptly, with big cat swiftness walking towards her.

'You dislike opposition!' she said very quickly, refusing to retreat but finding the effort almost intolerable.

'And you offer me some?' He stopped in front of her, his eyes moving over her face as if he had all the time in

140

the world. 'Even if you did, I can't change now, not for a green-eyed slip of a girl!'

'No, there's no fear of *that*!' Pain and a helpless kind of anger made her underscore him. A hit-because-you've-hit-and-you've-hurt-me desperation.

His hand closed over her shoulder, finding its delicate contours, hard conviction in his voice.

'I'd go carefully if I were you, little one. You have a decidedly odd effect on me!'

'I know I have!' The knowledge was almost too painful to be borne, but to have resisted him was quite beyond her. She swayed a little towards him, his thumb moving along her collarbone, inciting the sharpest yearnings.

'Don't be fooled by the too civilized approach,' he said a little grimly, his eyes on her mouth. 'Scratch the veneer and the polish barely goes skin deep. Remember that!'

She stared into his tautened face, the light striking flames from her hair. 'I'm not afraid of you, Rian!'

'A gallant denial, but why this little pulse?' His forefinger traced the blue little trip-hammer at the base of her throat, with a shivery destructive quality. 'If you're going to tell lies, you can't be too careful!'

'Don't *do* that!' she said almost pleadingly, her skin tightening electrically.

He took his hand away and the pain eased. His face softened with satire, a half ironic catch of laughter in his voice.

'Poor Rory! Torn by conflicting emotions and ruled by her head! But you know the old saying: All's fair in love and war! Let's call a truce. You try to be nice to me for a change, just a sweet, uncomplicated child, and I'll see what I can do for you in return!'

She flushed under that mocking gaze, so blatantly

insincere, and her eyes showed a jewelled flash.

'For the great Rian McCallum to stoop to bribery – I find that very distressing! What, no threats?'

His brief laugh silenced her. 'I haven't begun to threaten you. *Yet!* You're Bren's little girl-child, to be treated with great gentleness and respect!'

His face had a hard, disturbing charm, the glittery arrogance that wrought such a transformation in her. She stared up at him fixedly with a look of extreme temperament.

'It seems to me, Rory,' he said alarmingly soft, 'that you're being deliberately provocative.'

'Do you think so?' She moved towards him, but she seemed to be unaware of it. 'I might tell you I distrust you – profoundly!'

His face went rather grim. 'Do you think I don't know that? You know, Rory, you're rather a case, especially when you want to be made love to. I'm not such a fool that I don't know that!'

She jerked to a halt, a sleepwalker awake to hard fact.

'*You'll* never be invited to!'

He laughed under his breath, a saturnine cast to his face:

'*Invited?* God, I didn't think that necessarily applied, especially when you've got me the devil's apprentice. But you're right. You've got good reason to be frightened!'

'I'm sure of it!' she said with whispered intensity, pierced by the strange leaping lights in his eyes, intense and sensually alive. All her own inner conflicts were revealed in her face. Whatever she felt for Rian McCallum it was a floodtide that would surely sweep her out on to rocks. She had to escape! Some hidden reserve of spirit came to her aid.

'If you'll excuse me, Rian, I'll go find Tonia. She'd never forgive me for depriving her of a few moments of your time. She's been missing you, you know.'

He turned away from her casually and stubbed out his cigarette, his hard, lean body rippling with grace.

'All right, little one. Run away, while you can!' His voice was relaxed, self-assured, and suddenly she hated the sound of it, its power much too profound. She crossed the room like a dancer, her skirt swirling, wild to make her escape.

CHAPTER EIGHT

THE dinner dance was almost a disaster. If there was such a thing as a stage Irishman, Marc went to great pains to send up the immoral, amorous Italian, whose powers of seduction were never for one moment in question. With control he was very funny, but as the evening wore on, a bottle of wine and assorted drinks later, he was a sick headache, exuding passion, like an old Valentino movie.

Rory, who had grown fond of him, was inclined to be tolerant, but Tonia, very pretty and big-eyed in a scarlet silk jersey top with a gorgeous gipsy skirt, grew ludicrously tight-lipped, winning the approval of Kim, who had once been involved in a drunken-driver accident, needless to say through no fault of his own. Rory, looking at his smug, frozen face across the flowered centrepiece, found that the very qualities that had once attracted her were now weighing heavily against him.

'Beautiful women!' Marc was rhapsodizing in a progressively thick accent, although he had come out to Australia when he was seven years old. 'There is no food for thought like a beautiful woman. I find myself speculating about women all the time. Take our Rory . . . she affects no two men in exactly the same way!'

'I think we should be on our way,' Kim said repressively, his tone implying that they should never have come that way in the first place.

'Oh, please, *caro*!' Tonia covered his hand with her own. 'Don't take any notice of my so dreadful brother. He is a devil, a *demon*! He is doing this on purpose and it's not funny, Marco!' She shot her brother a wrathful look. 'Why, the night has only begun. I haven't danced half enough!'

'As long as my eyes have tears I shall weep for you!' her brother said soulfully.

'Rory?' Tonia looked away from her brother with open contempt. 'What have you to say?'

'I think I have the solution. I don't want to spoil anyone's evening, but I have an awful head — quite staggering, in fact. A lesser woman would have given up long ago. Marc can run me home and come back for you. It should clear his head!'

'Perhaps we should all go!' Kim said manfully in a halfhearted voice.

'No, please!' Rory held up a vaguely ironic hand. 'Marc, will you take me?'

'But of course, *poverina*! It is I who am guilty. But since you're all stuck with me I'll be back in about an hour. It will take me all of that!' He settled Rory's short jacket over her shoulders. 'My beautiful one, how I hate to see you suffer!'

She smiled a little, seeing in his eyes a sudden quick concern. 'I'm grateful for your sympathy, Marco, but let's go!'

Once off the highway, Marc put his foot down. He was driving mechanically, with both windows down to let in the night air. The panorama of canefields, lofty trees, crouching shrubs, a silver sickle moon, flashed by. It was a long straight run and Rory watched the needle go up to seventy. She murmured something vaguely repressive and Marc glanced briefly at her profile and checked back to fifty. She let her head fall back against the head rest. It was thumping in earnest now. Marc was talking very seriously and soberly for the night air had cleared his brain. About Kim he was inclined to be acid, informing Rory that it would be a 'ghastly waste of her womanhood' if she married one such as he.

Rory, inclined to agree, said nothing, so that gradually it dawned on Marc that she had withdrawn into her own private thoughts.

'You're miserable, *cara*!' he said softly. 'Forgive me, and I don't add to the joy of your expression!' He too fell silent, concentrating on his driving, straining his eyes through the darkness. The road spun away under the humming tyres. The car was moving swiftly now. There was nothing in sight, nothing to warn them of what was to happen next.

The off front wheel dropped off the road into the spread gravel. There was a raw, tearing sound, a shrieking blend of noises that mounted to a high-pitched scream. Rory lurched forward, braced by her seat belt, hitting the top of her head, not forcibly, on the windscreen before bounding back into her seat again. She fought for safety and equilibrium in a rocking world. Everything was happening almost too quickly for panic.

Adrenalin poured into Marc's veins. He switched off the engine, gripping the wheel hard, going with the skid until gradually he was able to straighten out without a compensating skid to the other side. The swirling dust and flying stones settled and the world regained its normal pattern. He brought the car to a shuddering stop.

'Mother of God and all the Saints! Are you all right, Rory?' He swivelled his compact body towards her, his hands still glued to the wheel as if it would take an operation to prise them away.

She touched her head gingerly. 'I think so! There's a bit of a bump on my head, but nothing to signify. At any rate, my hair will hide it!'

Marc let go the steering wheel with a visible effort, separating his fingers and holding them up. 'I must admit to a bad moment – a skid at sixty! Ah well, one less boy and girl angel for the next world, and I hear they're in need of them. It's the great miracle we had our seat belts on!'

'It's the law, you mean!' she pointed out soberly. 'I always wear mine.'

Marc shuddered and looked back over his shoulder, imagining the long, swerving skid marks, the perfect S burnt into the road. 'It's really much better to be born lucky than rich! Take it from one who knows, *cara*. You know, I feel completely sober. In fact I could sit and listen with great earnestness to a sermon. Are you well enough to continue, *cara*? You've been so good about this. My not-so-angelic sister would have been in hysterics by this or belting me about the ears!'

'Well, seeing I can manage neither, we'd better go on. Only this time try and keep up on the road!'

Marc had the grace to colour a little. 'I'm so sorry, *piccola*, this is dreadful – and what of your poor head now? I shall have to carry you in and tuck you in your little bed!'

'You *won't*!' Rory said much more in her natural tone. 'So far so good! Now drive on, and this time I'll sit up and pay attention.'

Rory never remembered very clearly the rest of the ride to the house. Marc helped her out of the car, holding her shoulder, looking into her face, speaking sympathetically, and she answered like an automaton, standing back from the low slung sports car as it reversed, watching the big, circular brake lights wink from the curve of the drive. She stood for a moment longer, swaying a little. A night bird swished softly by with its lost, forlorn cry, a curlew. She shivered in her thin gown, her nostrils assailed with the heavy, sweet scent of the wild wattles, her imagination conjuring up a vivid

147

mental picture of hundreds of fluffy yellow-gold constellations waving on the wind.

Somehow she was inside the house. The terrace lights were still on, flooding the garden, as they would until everyone was home, but the big chandelier in the entrance hall was out. Only the wall brackets showed a golden shower of light. The study was still ablaze, the door slightly ajar. There was no sound from within, yet Rory had the certain notion that someone was working inside. Instinctively she clung to the wall, crossing soundlessly to the stairs. She felt very pale and shaken, so probably she looked it as well. Her father would only be distressed by her appearance and want to know the cause of it. She simply didn't feel up to discussing it, let alone revealing in the process that the man she had once contemplated marrying had not seen fit to accompany her home. Her father wouldn't understand it. She didn't understand it herself, much less care about it. And that in itself was in the nature of a small shock. Kim Barrett, in a very short space of time, had come to mean next to nothing to her. Which just went to show what remarkable judgment she had.

She had just reached the bottom rung when she heard her name called, crisp, authoritative.

'Rory!'

She froze with wide startled eyes, a hapless doe with the hunter not far behind. In the next second her veins were filled with a mad impulse to pretend she hadn't heard and race up the stairs. But it was too late, and now she was wide open to a late-night interrogation, a remorseless third degree, and knowing Rian wasn't that what it would be?

He towered in the open doorway, the light behind him, raying out into the hall. His glance was comprehensive, surprise in every taut line of him.

148

'I thought I caught a glimmer of green. If I lived to be a thousand, Rory, you'd still have the power to startle me. Where the devil did you spring from, and where are the others?'

'Oh, please, Rian!' she said in a pathetic little voice, only faintly exaggerated.

His cool stare hardened and he lifted his hand rather cruelly to the light switch. The chandelier showed a million diamond prisms spilling its brilliant light all over her. She could have cried. She could have sunk right down on the step and cried.

'Well!' his voice plainly said: that settles it! He could see now her extreme pallor, the brilliant dilated eyes, the quick rise and fall of her slight breasts. Her bright head drooped on its slender neck. It was ridiculous, she told herself, to let him unnerve her the way he did.

'Good God!' he exploded with soft violence, more shivery than a shout. 'What's happened *now*? You're deathly pale. Where are the others? You'd better tell me quick!'

'Please, Rian!' she said huskily in a soft, ineffectual voice, her hand going to her throat. Anything at all was a shield against him.

A dangerous light flickered in his eyes and he shrugged his powerful shoulders. '*Please, Rian! Please, Rian!*' he mimicked her with extreme irritation so that in a sudden panic she turned about poised for flight.

He closed the distance between them with shocking speed, his hand at her waist as though her slightness and pale defencelessness was almost too much to be borne. She was almost on a level with him, her eyes on the cleft in his chin. He looked so immensely strong and vital, it was all she could do not to lean forward against him and calmly announce that she was there for the duration. The wild bent of her thoughts was so pitiful it was funny. She gave an odd little smile and let her lashes, thick and heavy, veil her eyes from him.

'Tell me!' he said, a variety of some primitive emotion prowling in his silvery eyes.

'Why, there's nothing to tell!' she said a little desperately, his hand at her narrow waist burning into the flesh. 'I had a headache, that's all!'

'A headache?' His winged black brows shot up in patent disbelief. 'Don't tell me you go as white as a sheet when you have a headache. That I simply won't believe even allowing for the stories you women concoct. And where in sweet hell is your fool of a would-be fiancé, if we must mention him?'

Her head dropped disconsolately like a tired child.

'I'm immune to all this, Rian, I really am. You'll just have to believe me. I didn't want to spoil anyone's evening, so Marc brought me home. Now he's gone back again to pick them up!'

His white teeth snapped together with exasperation. 'You didn't want to spoil anyone's evening! Now isn't that too touchingly sweet? You know, Rory, for a grown girl, you make me grit my teeth, and there's not a bit of use trying to reason with you. Did it occur to you no man worth his salt would have let you come home by yourself?'

'I didn't! I didn't! I *told* you. Marc brought me back!'

He drew a deep breath as if he didn't trust himself to speak, then he put out his hand to her as if to a captive bird. 'Come into the study anyway. You could do with a shot of something to settle your nerves. After a while you might consider telling me what's going on. I'll find out if I have to go out to the Country Club myself!'

She took the hand outstretched to her, trembling a little. 'It's really none of your business, Rian!'

'The hell it isn't!' he said forcibly, his eyes licking over her.

Sparks seemed to be flying from their joined hands. 'I wish you wouldn't swear at me all the time,' she said faintly. 'You're so forceful . . . so dominating!'

'It has its compensations sometimes and you damn well know it!' In the space of a second he swung her up into his arms, holding her still as if she were a child dead set on defying him. But she didn't want to. She didn't want to at all. She shut her eyes and relaxed against him, strangely willing to accept any ministrations he would offer.

He looked at her a little oddly, then walked with her back into the study, laying her down on the plush black leather sofa against the far wall. Rory let her spine relax against its thick upholstery lost in a languorous trance, her creamy pale face utterly still. She was safe in this dream world so long as she didn't open her eyes. She was safe, quite safe, with Rian McCallum blocked out.

'Rory!'

Wonder of wonders, his voice sounded quite gentle, the type of voice one used to charm birds out of trees, but she didn't open her eyes.

'No, I don't want anything!' she said politely, little girl fashion. 'I just want to lie here for ever! Where's Father?'

'He's gone off to bed. He seemed a bit played out to me!'

She frowned to hear her own opinion seconded. 'And Leonora?'

'She came in well over an hour ago. We had a night-cap together, then she went upstairs, and if you're going to ask where I am, I'm still here and I'm not going!'

'I don't care!' she said with startling honesty. His low laugh sounded in her ears. 'Well, that's news anyhow!

Sit up, Rory, you're having this!'

She could feel him above her. In another minute she was brought upright, his hand hard at her back, sitting beside her while she accepted the crystal tumbler with its scant amber contents.

'Drink it!'

His voice had that crisp, autocratic note that always squared her shoulders. 'You're a tyrant!' she said protestingly.

'I'm that all right!' he agreed with asperity. 'Don't sip at it like my old maiden aunt, *drink* it!'

She gave him a burning little glance, then tilted the glass, tossing off the contents as she had seen her father do. Not surprisingly she paid for it, gagging, the tears coming into her eyes so that they shimmered like lakes.

'Dear, oh dear, oh dear!' she murmured, appalled, filled with self-pity. 'What was *that*? Cold poison?'

'Remy Martin!' he corrected. 'An acquired taste, my child. But it will fix you up, don't worry. Lie back for a minute, then you can tell me what happened. Marc hasn't been acting up, by any chance? I know he's currently enamoured of red hair and green eyes!'

'Absolutely not!' she said emphatically.

'I thought as much, but it never hurts to check out every angle. So what else is it?'

She lay back, her hair spilling over the dull gold cushion, and shut her eyes again with a small sigh.

'I'll tell you nothing, Rian. You'll get nothing at all from me!'

'I wouldn't say that,' he drawled lazily. 'Your colour is coming back – that's one thing. How do you feel?'

'Floaty!' she murmured, her words totally inadequate to describe how she really felt. 'Ethereal!' she tried again, but it was nothing like that, a dull burning excitement was creeping through her veins, warming every inch of her. 'The only thing that's spoiling things is you!' she said lightly.

'Oh? Am I doing the wrong thing? Or to put it another way, why am I doing the *right* thing? You're a beautiful girl, Rory, in just the way I like – elegant, fastidious, intent on keeping distance between us, except for tonight!'

'Don't try to fascinate me, Rian McCallum!' she said hardily.

'Why not?'

'Because every intuition warned me about you, long ago!'

He leaned forward and traced the curve of her mouth with his finger.

'What bright spirit impelled towards delight was
ever known to finger out the cost?'

'Don't, Rian!' she said faintly, a million shivers running down her spine.

'Don't?' His laugh was a deep vibrant bell in his throat. He slid his arm under her back and pulled her into his arms, looking down into her upturned face, not pale now but pulsing with colour, heightened awareness. 'I've been promising myself this. The last time was like crushing a flower, but now! ... You're not quite so frail . . . so vulnerable!'

It was a curious moment, timeless, intense, yet suspended for Rory in a strange void. Then countless bitter-sweet sensations and impressions began to commingle, crowding into her mind: the crystal clear depths of his eyes, the faint glimmer of gold that overlaid his dark skin, the exact angle and cleft of his chin, the clear cut of his mouth. Behind his dark head, a copper vase thrust up lilies in a waxy, pale haze and to the side of it an ivory goddess watched them with long, inscrutable blind eyes. The scented night breeze sighed gently through the windows, swirling about them in soft eddies, jasmine and honeysuckle and the heavier more pungent scent of the bush wattles.

A faint smile touched her mouth and the light from the tall standard lamp gleamed on her brow, the fine curve of her cheek. She was breathing deeply, her eyes locked in his. His expression hadn't altered, but the changes in him, cataclysmic, existed in her senses, a knowledge and an awareness that linked them more powerfully than words would ever have done. Everything about him was so new yet so painfully, so disturbingly familiar, and he excelled at this curious waiting game, the bizarre touch. But she was not seeking now to deny or reconcile the irreconcilable, caught in the quicksand of the senses. He might almost have been waiting for her to make the first, the irrevocable move. Notions, all kinds of notions, began to filter through her brain, a kind of self-hypnosis, and her mouth softened and each separate feature was enhanced by sensual significance.

'Kiss me, Rian!' she said very softly, accepting without question that this was how it was to be.

His eyes were very steady, moving over her face, the brilliant liquid eyes, the delicate flare to her nostrils. He traced a fine line over her bare arm to her wrist. 'Are you begging, my so elusive, so exclusive Rory?'

'Yes!' she said gently, very feminine, yielding, desperate to be reassured.

He was suddenly something else, taut, very urgent, his hand tipping her head back arching her throat. 'You'd never have to do *that*! There's only one way this can end up!' He lowered his dark head and it was like night descending, with the stars, a million sparkling fragments.

It wasn't at all like the first time . . . the hunger, but not the pent-up anger, the elemental antagonism that had driven them then. Nothing mattered to Rory than that it was overwhelming, immense, instilling a frightening desire to be as close to him as she could get. Her pale arms reached up and wound around his neck, drawing him back with her so that her head came to rest on the crushed velvet cushion.

She could feel her heart fluttering, wanting it, yet marvelling that it should be so. She didn't know that she had abandoned pretence. Caring intensely, like an awakening from long winter's sleep. All she knew was . . . it was intoxicating, a sweet, burning release. A risk to be taken, without regrets. It was a night that would never end, a mainspring, a maelstrom of emotion that was the beginning of love.

She said his name softly, as if in a dream, her mouth seeking his, very young and ardent, her slender young body warm and smooth and alive, for he had power over her now, the natural advantage of driving masculinity and years of experience. But he knew it. He straightened abruptly, brought her upright with one inflexible movement, keeping his hand on the satiny skin of her upper arm, the only memento that remained.

She looked bereft, utterly disorganized, never more lovely. Her eyes shimmering, her lips parted, throbbing with warm blood. The glowing dark red of her hair spilled wildly about her flushed face, her body and spirit fused into one. It was the real Rory who stared back at him, volatile, emotional, wanting to be loved, eclipsing her self-contained shadow. For some reason it seemed important to her to see his eyes. She tilted her head to stare into his face. She tried to say something, her lips quivering, but he laid a finger over her mouth.

'No, don't say anything, little one. And don't try to

find an explanation for the inexplicable. You'll never find it. Accept it! And one more thing, get rid of Barrett, or I shall!'

She drew a jagged little breath, the light moving along the lovely curve of her breast. The nearness of him was exquisite, so much so that it was frightening. He drew her gently to her feet – as if she might shatter like glass, she thought wonderingly, knowing herself capable of anything. But his face was curiously empty, enigmatic, self-contained. He was a puzzle, a pleasure and a pain. It was all so baffling. His thumb unconsciously caressed the delicate hollow of her shoulder, then moved to smooth the tumbled disorder of her hair.

'Go to bed, Rory, like a good girl!'

The stunning change in his manner from the blinding rapture of a lover to a mentor was too much for her to comprehend. She looked up at him with all her small torments blazing in her face.

'I don't understand!' she said in a helpless, inadequate voice.

'Yes, you do!' he said briefly, the hard, glittery look back on him and no power on earth to change it. 'Now go along as I said. No fuss!'

She cast a last look at his dark impassivity, for the first time, stormy, rejected, a little overwrought.

'I shan't sleep at all!'

'You will!' He smiled and the smile reached the clear depths of his eyes. She turned swiftly away from him at right angles flicking the hair from the nape of her neck as if with the gesture, she too, was dismissing him.

'Good night, *Svengali*!' she said in a choked little voice, then flew on silent feet up the stairs, his aura clinging to her through every pore in her skin.

CHAPTER NINE

GETTING rid of Kim was a great deal easier than Rory ever supposed. Together they walked down to the canefields to watch the swift dispatch of the harvested cane to the mill, and there in the hot sunshine Rory told him, her young face intense, suffering a little, not wanting to hurt him but seeing no help for it.

'You're frigid, you know!' Kim turned on her with the stunning male opinion, a dreary obstinacy, supervirulent. 'It's as simple as that and no vague suspicions. It may not be exactly illegal, but it's inexcusable in a marriage. Never mind, dear, there's no more need for you to feel so self-sacrificing. You won't mind if I turn my attentions to Tonia? I can't take any responsibility for you!'

For a moment Rory had the mild impulse to slap his face, but it just as suddenly died on her. It was clear that Kim had a legitimate grievance. 'No,' she said in faint amazement blinking at his averted profile, 'but it would seem rather an odd thing to do!'

'Naturally you'd think so!' he said in a tight, barely audible voice. 'But it's my certain guess Tonia would prove an eye-opener after you. One can't court an iceberg for ever. You've no idea how expensive failure can be!'

Rory said nothing for a moment, then rose to her feet, seemingly engrossed in watching the giant red harvester making a debacle of all but the last field of cane, then she looked down at Kim still sitting on the grass, his face very pale. Her heart shrank a little and her voice softened. 'I should warn you, she imagines herself in love

157

with Rian!'

He looked up at her sharply, then laughed as if she had made a joke of Tonia's childish fancy. 'Rian? Oh, McCallum! Well, more fool she! My God, I thought she had more sense. Why, she's no more to him than a pretty child. Anyone can see that!' His blue eyes sparkled in the sunlight. 'I can see it will be worth my while to chat Tonia up!'

Something was aching at the base of Rory's throat and she pressed a hand to it instinctively. 'Well, do so by all means, and good luck to you,' she managed indifferently. 'I'm sorry if I hurt you, Kim. Believe me, I didn't intend it this way.'

Kim shook his blond head. 'You take yourself too seriously, darling. You haven't hurt me at all. You've hurt yourself. It's very likely for all your beauty, you'll go to an old maid's grave. Not that it's at all likely to matter!' He waited for a moment then said in an odd, brittle voice: 'I suppose you've told the whole beastly lot of them?'

'No, of course not!' Rory burst out roughly. 'It's not my intention to humiliate you!'

'Forgive me if I don't see that clearly! I'll tell you now, I intend to concentrate my attention on Tonia. She's desirable enough and it should make a pleasant change. If I'd used my head before this I would have seen she's far more what I need. Dating you was like drawing a blank every time!'

'Well, I shouldn't worry about it,' she said soothingly. 'There doesn't seem any point in prolonging this conversation, Kim, though I've learnt a great deal about myself I can work on. Please don't bear me any ill-will, Kim. I had to be honest with you and with myself!'

Kim closed his eyes. 'Well, thank you very much! But

let's leave it, shall we? I quite see that you can turn it on and off like a traffic light!' He was standing too, gritting his white, even teeth. The sun emphasized his sullen expression making him look very blond and cold. 'You know, Rory, you look like a woman, passionate, responsive, yet you act like a bright girl of ten. Ah well, sit in your glass bubble for the rest of your life. Actually, I'm grateful to you for putting paid to a life of frustrations. Just see you keep your lovely news to yourself until after I've gone. I don't want that fool of a Marc passing any snide remarks!'

Rory thrust on her sunglasses. 'I don't think he'd do that. You see, Kim, Marc is not unkind – not at heart. And if anything comes of your friendship with Tonia, which I doubt, you'd do well to remember she dearly loves her brother with all her warm Italian heart. And she *is* Italian, Kim. Her mother is. Her father was. Her children will very likely have great dark eyes and a glossy cap of curls. I'd find it enchanting myself, but I've surprised in you an odd kind of discrimination. My father as the head of the family would never tolerate it. Not for one instant!'

'Oh, set your mind at rest!' Kim said a little too quickly. 'I could well overlook all that, especially if a nice little dowry came along with her. Who knows, your father might leave her some property – Belguardo. I don't fancy it will go to Marc.'

Rory shook her head in silence, looking at and through him with peculiar penetration. 'Belguardo will never be Tonia's, and Tonia will want a real man. Whatever else you are, Kim, you're not that!'

'Well, that winds it up, then, darling,' Kim said in a strained voice, wiping the palms of his hands against his pale slacks.

She bit her lip, and bent her head. 'It looks like it, yes.

So far as I'm concerned I'll do or say nothing to embarrass you for the few days you have left. Tonia, of course, is free to make up her own mind. She seems to enjoy your company!'

'Well, you won't mind if I go find her, then!' Kim retorted with acid dignity. 'Strictly speaking, we should have had a violin obbligato through all that. You'll always remain a fascinating puzzle to me, Rory, but your big problem is you don't want it solved!' He whipped out his own sunglasses and stuck them on his nose. 'I can see you want to get rid of me. I go on Friday – and I'm not even sure you'll have to wait until then. Only don't ask me to ever kiss you again. The more common and conventional way, and the way that seems to appeal to you most, is to shake hands!'

Rory stood staring after him, in a semi-trance. Then she laughed, and once started she laughed for a long time, not unmixed with a few tears, wondering if every last emotion a man and woman felt for each other was, in the end, phoney! She sank down on to the grass again, watching with one part of her brain the huge mechanical harvester chop at the giant grasses like scissors. After a while she felt quite calm with a tremendous sense of relief that it was all over. At the very least, she was certain she wasn't frigid, but it wouldn't help Kim to know that!

In the end, Kim stayed the full length of his visit, and if any member of the household suspected the new situation between them, no one made mention of it. Only once in passing did Leonora pat Rory's cheek, her lustrous dark eyes holding shade upon shade of meaning and understanding. Certainly it helped, and Rory was grateful for her stepmother's calm reticence.

The farewells were brief but pleasant and Rory drove

Kim to the airport, stopping the car on the way home to cry her heart out, although she could not have said why, unless it was the senseless futility of a lot of human relationships. She arrived back at Belguardo very subdued and went to bed early, for in the morning Leonora and her father, Rian and herself were flying to Cairns for the weekend at the invitation of the Game Fishing Club. The season was right at its peak and Rian had already chartered a boat with its skipper and crew for the two days they would be there.

The town was full of rich Americans, Europeans, quite a few New Zealanders, the tobacco growers from the Tablelands, even a B.B.C. television crew, so that between the lot of them it was established that the blue deep off the Reef beat Panama, Peru, the U.S., South Africa, Canada, Mexico, Venezuela, the Bahamas and Colombia hands down. It was a rich man's sport, with the world marlin record held by an American who had spent an astronomical sum landing his fish.

The locals were very blasé about all this, contenting themselves with watching the daily dusk ceremonies when the fleet came in, some boats flying the red and white marker flags indicating that they had caught fish and thrown them back, a few flying the prized white flag with the black silhouette of the marlin. It was the tourists who became wildly enthusiastic, professing to think nothing of the initial outlay of seven thousand dollars for reel, dacron line, belts, gloves, sea harness, lures, everything in fact but the boat. That came on top. But the atmosphere was gay, rather lackadaisical, with time, everyone's friend!

Rory, strolling around the town in the morning before they went out, found it enchanting; the deep blue sweep of Trinity Bay before her and as a backdrop, the sharp clear line of the ranges slashed and softened by the Barron Gorge. Cairns was the Sun Capital of the Far North, warm all the year round, serving the rich cane-lands with its giant sugar terminal; the timber and the beef, the tobacco and the agricultural wealth of the hinterland. It had a lovely natural setting with its white municipal offices, cool white fluted columns, waxed floors and wide verandahs, rolling green lawns, the traveller's palms, the great fig and banyan trees, the mile-long esplanade fronting on to the Coral Sea, lined by soaring palms and the magnificent poincianas that would blossom with the monsoon. It was a tourist's mecca with palms and parrots, the air as soft as a flower, the sun a bright golden glory, with fish of all kinds abounding in its waters, delicious coral trout and bar-ramundi for the table.

Before they went out Leonora, strikingly attractive in navy slacks with an expensive navy and white silk-knit, came to Rory's room and together they swallowed a few pills to prevent seasickness, though Rory was reasonably certain she would be all right, being in general unaffected by motion sickness. Not so Leonora, who had sacrificed her own inclinations to please her husband. At least, on the first day out!

All the way to the harbour, Brendan Sheridan kept up a steady stream of talk, bright and relaxed in colourful holiday gear, wanting nothing better than a few days' break. So apparently did Rian, who was prepared to take it all as it came, his light eyes moving over the two women with cool, masculine appreciation. Out in the boat it was a crystal world, hand-cut by the gods. In their wake the town with the sentinel ranges, an unbelievable bluish purple and dead ahead, flashing its shot silver brilliance to the sky, the great sapphire sweep of the bay. There was no wind from the land, no racing white-flecked waves, no cloud on the horizon, only a shrieking tangle of sea-birds overhead.

Rory found she loved the water, the caress of the sea breeze, and her pleasure and excitement showed in her face so that her father, watching her, came to stand beside her with his arm around her shoulder, hugging her close. The sea was his great love, and it was obvious his daughter had inherited it.

In the wheelhouse, Leonora and Rian, relaxing while he could, chatted with the skipper, Leonora holding a long frosted drink tinkling with ice. Today she had a glimmer of her daughter's vivacity and an unaccustomed flush mantled her magnolia skin. Inwardly Rory applauded her, for she knew Leonora was rather frightened of boats and deep water. Not that there was any real risk, but the fear was there all the same. In the same way Rory hated lifts or the sensation of being closed in.

A few hours slipped by and in the way fish had, they didn't appear to be biting to order. They had spotted cruising sharks and a school of porpoise, but not the big kingfish. Lunch was an informal affair, leisurely, enjoyable, spiked by a sea appetite, and in the middle of it Giano, the bearded young deckhand, whispered hoarsely:

'Marlin astern!'

It was like throwing an electric switch. One moment they were all sitting there, lazily discussing their chances, and in the next moment Brendan Sheridan was on his feet, shoving his partner into the chair.

'Go on, Cal! Land the first one!'

Rian needed no more encouragement! Where seconds before there had been no more than a silver ripple a thin, black fin, facile and frightening, cleaved the blue sea like a bolt of shot silk. It was bearing down on the stern with astonishing speed, like some great torpedo. It skipped once in the wake, then it was gone. Lost to them?

Rian didn't think so. He gave a few terse orders over his shoulder and the skipper set a slightly curving course after the big fish. The line whistled out, only this time the marlin came half way out of the water and jumped the bait, crashing back into the ocean with a tremendous splash like a depth-charge. Rian braced himself for the shock of the bite, a solid wrench, which, if played with the arms, could nearly tear them out of their sockets. His full strength was concentrated in his long legs, for no man in the world could wind against the pressure of the diving giant.

The water was churning and boiling around the frantic fighting fish.

'If you're going to lose him, lose him right away!'

'The hell I will!' Rian couldn't spare the time to look at his partner. 'I've let him have the full spool. The hook's sunk sure enough!'

After a minute or two it seemed certain it had. The blue marlin jumped a few times clear of the water, a riveting spectacle, with runs of about one hundred yards in between. Its bulk glittered in the sun, pale blue belly, dark blue back, piggy eyes looking out at them wrathfully. The men seemed elated. It had to be well over the thousand pound mark! Rory could feel the deck vibrating under her feet, the excitement in her intense. The sun seemed to be gaining in strength by the minute. Rian was swearing gently, gritting his teeth, his powerful shoulders heaving while the skipper, a bronzed, whippy individual, crisped out his orders to the crew. The big game fishing had made a rich man of him. He had four boats now and the best clients. McCallum was sure to land this one. It would make the papers by the morning and do him no harm in the process.

For over fifty minutes the fight went on with Rian in the harness chair, from the expression on his vivid, dark face . . . tireless, exultant. What strange creatures men were, Rory thought, swallowing on a lump of excitement. As Rian slid forward the rod tip went down and as he pushed back with his strong legs braced, the rod tip came up, letting the drag of the line tire the big marlin. The kingfish made one last prodigious leap clear of the water, taking two hundred whistling feet of reel at a stretch, then it smashed back into the sea and spiralled up foam which soaked the deck with sea-spray.

'Hold him, son, he can't last much longer!' Brendan Sheridan shouted encouragement. 'I'd give my eye teeth to pull a beauty like that in!'

Ten minutes later it was all over and the giant fighting fish was strapped along the side of the boat, its head to the stern, its colours surprisingly brilliant but soon to fade.

The skipper looked his pleasure as he slapped Rian on the back.

'Congratulations! No risk about it, it should go eleven hundred at least!'

Rian eased himself out of the chair to stand up tall, stretching his long arms a little gingerly, still quivering from the strain, looking down at the raw blisters on his hands, then he turned his dark head to where Rory was standing staring at him, hectic apricot sun-spots on her high cheekbones. He reached forward and caught the point of her chin, dropping a hard kiss on her mouth. She found herself responding, her mouth flaming.

'Hail the conquering hero!' he said vibrantly, his eyes extraordinarily brilliant. 'And if you really want to know, I feel sorry for the fish!'

'You do now it's over!' Brendan Sheridan laughed, his eyes moving from Rian to his daughter with a shock of interest. Then he turned and looked over the side at their magnificent catch, his expression frankly envious. 'There's little doubt we've got ourselves a big one. A season record at any rate. Good for you, Cal. Now it's my chance!'

Behind them the white flag with its leaping black marlin snaked up the mast with Giano, the gangling deckhand, glassy-eyed with excitement, outwardly speculating on the monster's great weight.

'Gee, I sure hope it takes a prize, Mr. McCallum. It's the biggest fish I've ever seen. It might even go to twelve hundred pounds!'

Leonora, smiling, but in no way as excited as the others, moved along to them with a celebration tray of drinks, touching her petalled mouth to Rian's cheek.

'Congratulations, *caro*! Such a pity we can't eat it!'

Rian smiled and said nothing as he tossed off his drink, and Rory could see plainly that it was all in a day's work to him. They fished for a few more hours unsuccessfully, until just before dusk, when the sky was a bright orange and her father landed a big one; an eight-hundred-pounder. He played it for forty minutes or so, his eyes gleaming, yet twisting in the chair trying to get comfortable. The straps were cutting into him and he was feeling the weight of the rod, the effort it was to keep upright.

Cal shouted down to him again and he smiled thinly, gritting his teeth. He was damned if he was going to lose it. It was the fish or him. But the fish was still slashing, fighting back, never tiring, and with a shock of dismay Brendan Sheridan realized he was a young man no longer. Already his back was acting up on him. Leonora, sensing something out of the ordinary, was beside him, a little anxious now.

'Don't tire yourself like this, Bren! Try again

tomorrow!'

'Don't fuss, my dear,' he answered lightly. 'Fishing's good fun, isn't it, Cal?'

For a few moments the marlin seemed to be drifting on the line and he relaxed his aching muscles, then with an almighty effort he jerked hard on the line, tempted in that final moment to be strong. He pushed back in his chair, getting all the help he needed from the wheel. His lips were stinging, the salt rough on his face. In that moment he forgot everything; his weariness and discomfort, the ache in his limbs, his cramped hands. He was going to land this fish. They would go in running not one but two white flags. He was tiring, but he had enough experience to pull it off. Possibly the fish had exhausted itself with those long runs and dives, for it was quiet enough now.

The reel suddenly squealed in anguish, the marlin leapt like a crazed thing, its jaws snapping, surfacing, smashing out with its tail, streaking like a deadly missile for the open sea and freedom, while Brendan Sheridan slumped sideways in a tight black knot of pain, then collapsed in his chair.

Rory lay on her back with only the sheet over her, the fluffy lemon rug in a ball at her feet. It was a few minutes now since she had floated back to consciousness, as the effects of the drug wore off. She gazed up at the pale clouds of tropical netting, her forehead pleating, trying to mesmerize herself into believing that that fierce, horrible little scene hadn't taken place. She shivered and put her arms around her. She was sure, quite sure Rian would never forgive her. She fought to control the ache in her throat. He was as proud as Lucifer. It was all or nothing with Rian. Once he had desired her as a woman, she knew that, but even that

167

slender advantage had been lost to her. A taut feeling welled up in her and she tried to stand away from herself, peering into what she really was. But it was hopeless. Her head was swimming. And what of her father, lying alone in a hospital bed?

Her eyelids stung with tears and she closed her eyes, letting them slide weakly down her cheeks and back on to the pillow. What was her life now? Two men, her father and Rian. Part of her now. She couldn't lose either of them. Her eyes flicked open at the sound of the door knob turning. Leonora entered, the light shining dully on her pale, beautiful face. It looked extremely grave, and Rory's heart gave a great lunge of fright and pain. Leonora, looking across to see whether her stepdaughter was awake, surprised the tear-bright glitter in those brilliant green eyes. She crossed to the bed swiftly, her voice low and compassionate.

'But no, *cara*, no, no, *no*! Your father is sleeping peacefully. Have no fear about that. God had been good to us. It was a heart attack, as we thought – not a bad one, but a warning for all of us. How are you, my poor child? We have had a bad time of it, you and I!'

Rory reached up a hand and Leonora clasped it, a fleeting smile on her face. Disarmingly she said:

'At last we shall take a holiday together, my husband and I. A long one – a long, *loving* one! The first in very many years!'

Rory moved her mouth, curling up like a kitten, visibly relaxing. 'Doctor's orders?'

'Very much so!' Leonora smiled. 'Bren has pushed himself too hard for too long. I have decided I don't want any more money. I only want my husband. Cal can take over the reins for as long as is necessary, and no one more competent. Then, when we come home, Marc will start pulling his weight. I shall see to it. You see, *cara*, sometimes a mother makes mistakes with the best intentions in the world. But in my case, not irretrievable ones. Both my children are goodhearted, goodnatured. They will respond to this new situation. My childhood was not easy, and I wanted it to be different for Marc and Tonia. But I overstepped the mark. One becomes as much accustomed to riches as poverty, but I shall redirect myself, you'll see!'

Rory sighed deeply. 'I was so frightened, Leonora. Do you understand how I behaved as I did? My reaction? though I know there's no possible excuse for it. It was a kind of breaking point, I think!'

Leonora smoothed the sash around her quilted silk robe, then began to pleat it lightly. 'I understand, child, but one can't help regretting . . .!'

'Don't say it, I *know*!' Rory's soft mouth quivered in distress. 'Strange how little we know of what's ahead of us. To start out this morning with such high hopes! A record catch!' She shrugged bitterly. 'Poor Father! Poor Rian! Poor me – poor *stupid* me! I'm so bitterly ashamed of myself!'

Both women fell silent, reliving a shocked moment at the hospital when Rory, like a small fury, had flown for Rian, floods of panic, and pain, and resentment racing through her veins. He looked so strong, so vital, and through the porthole window she could see her father . . . so grey, so prematurely aged, so helpless. It had been too much for her. It was all *his* fault – *Rian's*! Her father had tried to match a much younger man. She hated him. Hated him, very much afraid of what she would do. She had hit out at him frantically, beating her small clenched fists against him, hopelessly out of control while he held her. She still bore the imprint of his fingers – staring down at her coldly, the muscles of his jaw taut, a nerve throbbing in his temple, a white look around his nostrils proclaiming his steely restraint. Leonora, dark eyes wide with multiple shocks, trying to calm her, soothe her, begging her to have a care what she was saying, and all the time Rian holding her saying tightly: 'Let her go! Let her get it right out of her system!'

How he hated her for it, for she had got it out of her system, past caring, sobbing bitterly, all the pent-up tears of years of frustrations and exercising control. She could never lose her father, not now that she had found him again. The thought was too terrible to be borne. In the end they had given her an injection, Rian holding her arm, and the great weight was lifted from her heart and the strength in her limbs ebbed away.

But now she had returned to feeling and sensitivity and she could see that she might very well torment herself for the rest of her life. Leonora made a funny little sign of absolution over her head.

'Try not to distress yourself about it. You can only apologize and ask for Rian's forgiveness. He's devoted to your father, you know. It was as bad for him as it was for us, but men have a different way. Not a better way, I don't think, because they bottle so much up. There is much relief in tears. Come now, *cara*, please smile at me. Your face is so white!'

Rory looked up, smiling a little painfully. 'Please forgive me, Leonora, but I thought you had a tenderness for . . . for Rian!' It came out with a jerk and Leonora's full mouth looked ironic, but her eyes gleamed suddenly years younger.

'Perhaps I should learn to guard my glances, little one. Rian is a very striking man, I would be less than human if I failed to notice. Sometimes, you know, *cara*, a woman likes to feel herself attractive to a much younger man. It's just one of those odd little quirks you yourself

170

might experience one day. But harmless. Just a pleasant daydream hurting no one. Please believe me when I say your father is the only man I want for the rest of my days. But you do Rian an injustice, my child. He would have no such thought of me, surely you realize that? Rian is a man of the world – acute, very perceptive. He knows what women are like. It hasn't always been easy for me, you know, with your father so deep in his business affairs. He told me once, and only now, to-night, do I forgive him, that I married him as a meal-ticket! How I raged at him at the time! I think now he no longer believes it, for it was never true. I knew he would look after me well and the children because that was part and parcel of the man, but only a small part. I married your father because I loved him and needed him, his support and protection. I still love him, still need him – never more than tonight. When I left him I think he realized that. Who knows for the first time?' She gave Rory a long, speculative look. 'You won't mind if I take your father off for six months or so? Six long peaceful months of doing nothing. He'll probably chafe a little, but he'll get used to it!'

Rory suddenly smiled, illuminating her pale face with great charm and warmth.

'All I want for all of us is to be happy. Take Father by all means, with my blessing!'

Leonora leaned into the glow of the lamp and kissed her stepdaughter's cheek.

'It may yet happen, this happiness you speak of. Good night, *cara*. Things will be brighter in the morning!'

'Good night, Leonora. I'd like to think so anyway. I shall compose an apology and hope it will be received!'

Leonora walked to the connecting door of the suite, smiling wryly over her shoulder, her tall figure throwing up a shadow on the wall, her glossy black hair braided for the night.

'You look like one of those Greek figures on a Wedgwood urn,' Rory said wonderingly, fascinated by that proud head carriage.

'Never Greek, *cara*, *Italian*,' Leonora smiled. 'But I accept the compliment!'

The door closed softly, but Rory wasn't yet ready to go to sleep. She adjusted the bedside light. Lights were such reassuring things when one had a lot of things on one's mind. She needed comfort lying there for a long time thinking her own thoughts, then she drifted off. . . .

When she awoke someone was in the room. She turned her head, unalarmed, to see Rian neatly folding a note at the dressing-table, his back to her, his dark face reflected in the mirror. He thrust his pen back into the pocket of his jacket and turned towards her.

Immediately she lowered her thick eyelashes, feigning sleep. She lay rigid, debating whether to speak to him or not. She had her chance, but from the set of his dark head he wouldn't welcome any apology from her. Her eyelashes were fluttering and she only hoped he wouldn't notice them. She could feel his tall presence beside her at the bedside table. The impulse to speak to him was too much for her. Her eyes flew open and she reached out a hand to him.

'Rian?'

'Oh, you're awake!' He stood in front of her, very tall, very dark, a light-eyed, unutterably remote stranger. 'I've just come from the hospital. Your father is resting quite comfortably, doing well. We'll be able to take him home tomorrow afternoon.' He turned and picked up the note and handed it to her. 'It's all there in black and white. I thought you might like to know before you went to sleep!'

'Thank you, Rian.' At the touch of his hand she trembled, but he thrust his own hand into his pocket.

'No trouble!'

'Please, Rian!' Her eyes were shimmering, misted over, her hair with a life of its own springing back from her temples in a wild cascade over her bare shoulders. 'Don't be so cold with me. I can't bear it. I'm so terribly sorry for what I said. Won't you forgive me?'

Something like anger touched his face. 'No, Rory, I won't!' he said finally, his voice cool and cutting. 'You're not going to give *me* hell!'

'Rian!' She almost recoiled from him as if from a blow still compelled to look up into his face. 'Please try and understand. It was Father looking so drawn and helpless. You can't imagine how you looked in comparison. I've just found him . . . the thought of losing him . . . I lost my mother not so long ago,' she pleaded with him, almost crying. 'She was a strange woman, but I loved her!'

His brilliant eyes moved her face and shoulders with cold indifference. He looked hard and unforgiving and she loved him. 'Perhaps you've got more of her in you than I thought!'

'Perhaps I have,' she agreed quietly. 'But you might be over-simplifying a complex problem. Good night, Rian. Thank you for letting me know about Father.'

He walked away to the door without a backward glance. 'Good night, little one. Bren sent you his love. He was worried about you. I'm sorry I can't add my own!'

CHAPTER TEN

RORY stood on the terrace overlooking the floodlit gardens. The barbecue fires were blazing merrily, shooting out psychedelic lights; orange, red and gold, flares of electric blue, even slivers of palest jade. The harvest was over and Belguardo was a glitter of lights. Almost everyone in the district was there, wearing a party face, even the children, in their best clothes, weaving and bobbing, gone crazy with joy and being allowed up too late. Some of them, the tiny tots, were already asleep on the fluffy rugs and mounds of cushions under the silver trees that glittered with fairy lights. The post-harvest barbecue on Belguardo was an institution, never to be missed. The climate, the love of informality and the outdoors as well as the huge crowd made this form of entertainment ideal, so that Rory, looking out over her beautiful surroundings, was enveloped in a sense of pathos almost, an aching pressure at the base of her throat. This was Belguardo, her home.

The fires, so carefully built, made a glowing night-time spectacle, the focal point of any barbecue. There were long parallel lines for all the skewered cooking, whether meat, fish, poultry or the foil baked vegetables; wide open ranges for the freshly caught fish, the whole barramundi basted in a tangy sauce and grilled in their special racks with chopped herbs inside and slices of lemon arranged along their backs; the grilled prawns and bacon rolls, the carpetbag steaks and marinated T-bones, magnificent chunks of rump steak three inches thick served with baked-in-their-jackets potatoes and slices of avocado; the hibachi kebabs, very popular, with each person helping themselves with the ingredients that suited their taste; the red and green peppers, small onions, whole tomatoes, mushrooms and slices of pineapple. The children loved these, the idea of helping themselves, but the responsibility for the cooking lay in adult hands. For those who preferred chicken, charcoal cooked poultry roasted on the spit with all kinds of cooked vegetables gilded with butter and grilled. On separate tables the salads and dressings were set out, the sauces, the relishes and chutneys, the lashings of hot crusty garlic bread. There were kegs of icy cold beer, the only way Australians new or old would drink it, and gallons of *vino* and soft drinks for the children. The whole scene was one of colour and exhilaration and immense enjoyment.

Rory took a deep breath, willing herself out of her self-absorption. She had to meet Marco at nine o'clock and it was nearly that now. Tonia, black-eyed and blithe in a brilliant zebra print patio dress with someone dark and male caught up in tow, walked across the grass calling up to her:

'Has Cal arrived yet, *cara*? He has never been so late before!'

Rory leaned over the balustrade, the reflected light falling over her face and hair. 'I haven't seen him as yet. I did hear Father mention that he might be delayed for a bit.'

Tonia's companion was peering up at her rapt. 'You look like Juliet! You're not Juliet, are you? Tut! I have lost myself. I am not here. This is not Romeo, he's some other where!'

'Whose side are you on, Dario?' Tonia frowned over her shoulder at him.

'I *know*!' Dario continued, still staring up at Rory, the dark olive of his forehead pleating. 'You can only be the so beautiful addition to the family – Rory!'

'But of course!' Rory smiled. 'How are you, Dario?'

'Captivated, *nina*! I never expected to meet you.'

'Bye-bye, now, I'm taking him off,' Tonia said lightly, 'so there's no sense standing there awaiting developments, *cara*!'

Dario hunched his shoulders expressively. 'You are a mystery to me, Tonia. *Arrivederci, signorina.* I shall see you later on. I have some fascinating tales to tell! Much to offer a young girl!'

'I'm going *now*,' Tonia said again, and waved an airy hand before linking it through Dario's.

Rory lingered looking after them, watching them move across the springy grass on their way to the redwood seats and tables set out under the trees. She could see Marc in the distance lending a hand with the drinks. She still had a little time. She sighed and walked back inside the house, seeing across the space of the living-room the face of the man she loved: a thing of planes and shadows, so many different moods. He was smiling faintly, his lean cheeks creased, his dark head inclined, talking to her father. Her heart melted away. He looked so relaxed, so assured, so infinitely exciting. She moved forward. Like Tonia and Leonora, she was wearing a long hostess gown, only hers was in a swirling abstract pattern of amber, charcoal and gold, sleeveless with a deep V ruffled neckline and a wide belt at her narrow waist.

Rian looked up and saw her and she felt her nerves shrivel with apprehension. They had been avoiding each other, but her father, oblivious, beckoned to her. She moved across to them like a long-stemmed flower, smiling at the guests who spoke to her in between.

'Hello, Rian, how are you?' To look at him was to be

176

swept into an abyss, lost. She got it over with quickly, her eyes only lightly touching his, intensely aware of the dynamic energy that was so vitally a part of him.

'Never better, and you, Rory?' he answered idly, under the superficial goodwill a current of tension.

She murmured something appropriate, feeling very keyed up, released into new areas of pain. His eyes were moving lightly over her dress. She had no means of knowing whether he liked it.

If Brendan Sheridan was aware of the cross-currents he gave no sign, still smiling, looking with proud eyes at his daughter, her flushed flowerlike face.

'How's it going outside, darling?'

'Everyone seems to be enjoying themselves. Some of the children have fallen asleep under the trees. I suppose they'll spring to life in an hour or so ready to stay up all night!'

'They will for the dancing!' her father agreed. 'The Italian community put on a very good show!' He turned about and picked up a long book from the table behind him. 'I've just been showing Cal your sketchbook. I had no idea you were so good, my lamb. I particularly like the one of Leonora, head and shoulders. It's not easy to capture the essence of a person. I'd say you've done that. In fact, I've a mind to commission a portrait. How would you like that?'

She looked at him with a twinkle, her pulses slowing. They hadn't got very far! 'I'm not that good, Father!'

'There's no need to be too modest, Rory, though it's very refreshing!' Rian intervened. 'You have considerable ability!'

'Why, thank you, Rian!' she said lightly, her voice cool and rounded, every syllable distinct, but still not looking at him.

'I always like to encourage the young ones,' he rejoined suavely. 'Presumably you need a little. I didn't notice one of myself!'

'There goes another illusion!' Brendan Sheridan gave a soft chortle. 'Excuse me, you two, there's Reg Innis and his wife. I'll go have a word with them!' He moved off purposefully to where a middle-aged couple had just entered the room.

With a swift compulsive action Rory got hold of her sketchbook. She couldn't bear it a minute longer, though they hadn't got more than half way through. Rian's hand closed over the other end of the book.

'What are you hiding, Rory?'

'Nothing at all!'

'Let me see.'

'Damn you, Rian, I won't!' She gave an odd little out-of-character laugh.

His light eyes gleamed and his head tilted with customary arrogance. 'It's silly to make a fuss now, little one. Besides, I've seen it. No, don't look at me like that. It's true!'

'Well, you can't have it!' she said as calmly as she was able.

'You're ridiculous and you know it!' He took the sketchbook out of her nerveless hand and turned up all but the last page. 'Is that how you see me?'

'When I *like* you – yes!' He smiled at her with a half mocking, half caressing glance that swept her hopelessly to sea. 'But I haven't been seeing you, have I? You've made it perfectly clear where I stand.'

'You're seeing me now,' he said lightly, moving his eyes from the sketch to her face. 'I do believe you've lost a little weight. In fact you look rather breakable. A melancholy girl into woman. Highly caressable! Have you been unhappy, Rory?' His brilliant gaze searched for hers, though she tried to avoid it.

'About what?'

'What indeed!' His mouth twisted into a wry grin. 'Bren and Leonora leave on Wednesday. I was thinking of giving a little dinner party Monday night. Tuesday would be too late, I think!'

'Uum!' She nodded her glowing head noncommittally, taking the sketchbook out of his hand and staring down at the charcoal drawing; the exact mould of the features, the shadows at the corners of his mouth and nostrils, the arrogant curve of nostril and lip, the deeply cleft chin. It was very good, and what was more frightening, it communicated the urgency of all that she felt, the senseless, romantic yearnings. She dropped it as if it scorched, turning the cover up and folding it down with her hands.

'You might come and do the flowers,' he suggested lazily, his eyes, anything but indolent, watching her intently. 'You've never seen where I live. Aren't you curious?'

'Tonia told me you had a super-elegant bachelor pad. Apparently she was rather involved in helping you create it, or so she said!'

His expression turned into cool analytical detachment. 'No, Rory, I'm devoted to Tonia, as you know, but I did it all myself. Home therapy, or a labour of love. I think you just made that up in the hope of making me angry!'

'Is that so unusual?'

'No!' he agreed abruptly. 'It's a primary impetus with you. What more fun in life than lashing out at Rian? The main issue seems to revolve around accepting me for what I am, not what you'd like me to be. For I'll never change, not even if I'm taken over completely by a green-eyed witch with odd moods. No man exists as a pure type, Rory, we're all mixtures of this and that –

the good and the bad, the strengths and the limitations. How long have you been wanting to change me?' He was speaking so softly now he might have been talking to himself.

'It would take more courage than I've got!' she said gently.

'Stop playing around, little one. No pretence. Take your time. I'm listening!'

She looked at him undistracted with a stillness of the heart. She didn't want to change him at all. Once perhaps when he frightened her more than a little, but not now. He was Rian and she wouldn't have him any different. For a long moment she allowed herself the luxury of looking into the depths of his eyes, seeing her own reflection. They seemed to be alone in a room that was swirling with music and chatter and ripples of laughter.

His face seemed to tauten, his voice challenging. 'What is this, Rory? Seduction by remote control? Stop looking at me like that. I've only so much left by way of restraint!'

She was still looking at him intently, as if they were locked in a duel. 'You're so much better at this game than I am!'

'I know damned well I am!' he said with soft violence. 'Only this time I'm not playing. What's wrong, Rory, can't you take it?'

'Not here. This minute. In a room full of people!' she said jerkily in a soft husky voice, filled with the mad notion that she was being made love to.

He kept silent, then he laughed. 'It's a lovely thought! In my imagination I'm not treating you lightly!'

Excitement surged like a storm through her veins. It was far, far more important to get away from him now.

Marc, coming in from the terrace, caught sight of them and came on across the room, his dark, good-looking face bright with pleasure.

'How are you, *fratellino*? Why did no one tell me you were here, and what have you been doing to Rory? She looks almost frighteningly beautiful – a little wild, great glittery eyes and colour under the skin. What is it, this way of yours with women? I must know!'

'You've got *me*!' Rian said in a light ruminative voice. 'It might serve your own interests to show Rory what sort of a hand you are with a flaming kebab!'

Marc smiled and shook his glossy head with its thick deep waves. 'I see it! Mind your own business. Ah well, let's do what he requires of us, *cara*. I shall fill your plate and mine and we shall sit together in the garden. You'll be quite safe – he's made sure of that. Haven't you, Cal?'

The two men exchanged a long glance with Marc looking away first. 'Are you eating at all, *fratellino*?'

'Not for the moment, Marco,' Rian said easily, his glance flicking over Rory and away again. 'You two go along and enjoy yourselves. I'll be out later when the fun starts!'

By about midnight, most of the guests with young families had gone home, but there were still plenty of people about laughing, singing, dancing in groups. The Italian community were unquestionably experts at the particular task of enjoying themselves. Rory found herself strolling with Marc to the perimeter of the canefields where people were seated in rough semicircles listening to the music of the accordions and an undeniably virtuoso violin. Its solo voice soared, singing exquisitely over the lesser mortals, the accordions.

The faces in that lovely green setting reflected no

weariness, only pleasure and a faint nostalgia for the Homeland, faraway families, other scenes, days gone by. Rory's eyes roamed over the crowd, seeking, seeking. . . . Further off in a different group she found him, taller than the others, standing with one arm resting negligently on an acacia branch, the other holding a cigarette, the smoke wisping in front of his eyes. His pale shirt glimmered against his dark skin, the tiny black and white checkered jacket swung free.

Tonia was beside him, looking up into his face, her black eyes sparkling in the glare of the amber lights almost hidden in the trees, still powerful enough to dominate the whole area. Rian was smiling, saying something, his tall, loose-jointed elegance setting him apart. The music came to a halt and immediately the clapping broke out and calls for the traditional music the folk dances they all loved so much. The young people were on their feet, laughing, hands swinging, forming a circle.

'Come along, Rory!' Marc caught at her waist with warm, urgent fingers.

'Oh no, Marc, I can't manage those kind of steps. I'm a little tired!'

'You don't look in the least tired, only extravagantly lovely with so much colour in your face. Come on, *cara*, let's show them how to really dance!'

It was useless to protest. He drew her out on to the grass while the others clapped and shouted his name, parting to let them in. The violinist turned in Rory's direction, bowed, then with a splendid *appassionata* cadenza broke into a brilliant runaway dance tune with a melody unfamiliar to Rory, but it was irresistibly exuberant, vivacious and abandoned, executed with considerable violinistic skill, fully exploiting the instrument. Rory turned her head in stunned admiration, but everyone else was used to Ugo Marietti's mastery. The accordionists joined in with typical goodwill, unable to match the brilliance of the violin but swelling the volume of sound.

The music surged with its obvious gaiety, colouring the dancers' consciousness so that they were caught up in its spell, the women's skirts fluttering and swirling like butterflies, passing from partner to partner. A girl called Giulia suddenly ran lightly into the centre of the ring and began to dance with stylized grace, apparently oblivious to every other soul, then without breaking her step, pirouetted out of the circle into the arms of a young man, handsome, showy, with good features, white teeth and black hair, who gathered her up.

The violinist ran his bow up the strings and stopped, looking with pleasure around the gay festive scene, colourful, exotic, rather abandoned. Rory stood quite still, her hand over her racing heart, her eyes glittering like emerald chips, her hair in an auburn cascade around her flushed face. She had scarcely recovered her breath when the music started out again and her partner caught her hand, twirling her round so that she was circling the ring, her feet scarcely touching the ground. She was losing all sense of self-consciousness now; the breeze fanned her flushed cheeks, the fairy lights flashed out the deep reds of her hair and she abandoned herself to a sensation of utter weightlessness.

Shouts of laughter punctuated the night, rhythmic clapping from the onlookers, insistent, almost hypnotic, augmenting the sound of the accordions, the wizardry of the violin. Excitement was mounting to a crescendo point when suddenly she was being whirled into the darkness of the banyan trees, black as ebony. A young ardent voice was breathing in her ear, a dark face near hers, all squares and angles. 'Come now, my beauty,

183

bellissima, I won't hurt you! A kiss?' Warm lips were pressing down on her hair, his breath stirring it. '*Alla nazzarene!* A mass of flames – so beautiful!'

Rory thrust back against those strong imprisoning arms, looking up into a face that was little more than a smooth blur in the night.

'Don't!' she said breathlessly. 'I don't like it. Please let me go!'

'But you can't be so cruel! To see you dance!' The voice was extravagantly disappointed, softened by surprise.

'But *I* can!'

Rian suddenly materialized from nowhere, action implicit in his words, his tall, powerful frame. He got a hard hand on the young man's shoulder and spun him away with irresistible force. 'All right, *amico*, you can go back to the dance!'

'But I meant no harm!' the young man protested. 'It is a celebration, you understand!'

'We understand!' Rian murmured laconically. 'Now run along!'

Unexpectedly white teeth flashed with a complete lack of animosity. '*Mea culpa, signore.* I can see now that you could easily knock me down with a finger. It is not so very terrible to kiss a woman. And with *red hair!*' That important matter settled, the young man made off swiftly without a backward glance.

Rian turned to the silent girl with a calm, tranquil movement. 'Better late than never! Are you recovering from your little experience? It's the very devil to have red hair!'

His voice seemed to be mocking her, threaded with laughter.

'How was I to know I would be whirled away like that?' she asked with a flash of heat.

'My darling child, when these young hotheads get worked up they could have a passionate affair with a stick of furniture! And there you were flittering around like Isadora Duncan! What can you expect? It's not entirely his fault. Certainly no one else has what you've got!'

The soft drawl was like a prelude to laughter in his dark velvet voice.

'Well, thank you for rescuing me,' she said in hushed tones, trying to keep her temper.

'Didn't you think I would?'

'I don't flatter myself all that much!' She could see his head thrown up and his eyes gleaming, the merest lick of something out of the ordinary in his voice.

'Oh, come on now, Rory!'

'Now you're here, there's bound to be a catch in it,' she said with a funny little sigh.

'There is,' he agreed very smoothly. 'I want to talk to you. I'll never get another opportunity like this one!'

Something, some curious element, the timbre of his voice, the deceptive indolence of his tall lean body, made a child of her. She gave a muffled little exclamation and took to her heels on a reflex action, running headlong through the trees, her long skirt fluttering, the brilliant myriad stars in the clearing just ahead. Everything was working against her; the velvet dark, the night wind that caught at her hair, skeining it over her face. She stumbled a little, her nervousness transmuted to a queer rising fever. He caught her up easily, drawing her back into the hard circle of his arms.

'Don't struggle, you stubborn little idiot! I've been right about you all along!'

'Oh!' she said sombrely. 'You're a horrible man!'

His hands tightened about her rib cage. 'Rory, if you keep *that* up, I swear I'll never be friends with you again!'

The wind was at her hair again. She spun in his arms her hands lifting rather frantically to her tumbled hair, staring up into his dark face with wide, shining eyes.

'What is it you want, Rian?'

'Don't fight me and you'll find out!'

The deep note in his voice made her head reel. 'I won't be an interlude, an affair. I *won't*!' A clamour was rising in her, a passionate fury, yet she was leaning towards him with unconscious allure.

'Oh yes, you will!' He laughed in his throat, his hand clasping her nape, shaping it. 'Because I can't do without this physical magic!'

The impulse to resist him died like a flame. She turned up her mouth and he claimed it with consummate passion, such unquestioned possession that her heart leapt like a wild thing and excitement licked along her veins like fire. His arm was about her, crushing her to him. A loosened coil of her hair got between them and he lifted his hand and brushed it away, looking down at her pale creamy face, the heavy dark sweep of her fallen eyelids, kissing her mouth again with resistless mastery, a sensual technique that once had frightened her. Now it was an ecstasy, a golden, irresistible tide.

Her words came like a soft sigh against his mouth.

'Rian?'

'Hmmm!' He scarcely seemed to hear her, tipping her chin up to kiss her throat.

'I love you!'

The caressing hand stopped. 'You're in love with me, Rory. You don't *love* me. But I'm going to take unfair advantage of that. I'll never let you go – never! So rid yourself of any idea of that!'

'But you've been so remote . . . unbending . . . since I

. . . since . . . !' Her voice quivered and cut out, unwilling to broach the subject ever again.

'What I feel for you would withstand any threat,' he said a little roughly. 'But don't ever do it again or I'll make love to you in a way you're not likely to forget!'

'I only wish you would!' she said with soft, husky, urgency, leaning towards him to trace a gentle finger over the cleft in his chin. She might have a son with a chin like that.

He caught her hand and kissed it, holding her away from him, riding himself on a tight leash. 'You're a provoking child, Rory, but people who make love under the stars either don't want anyone to know about it or they've nowhere else to go. When I make love to you as I want to . . . and I'm going to . . . there'll be no flaw in anything. The time, the place, the setting, and you'll be Mrs. Rian McCallum. There's just no other way. How long do I have to wait?'

'Months!' she said in an odd little voice, only faintly teasing.

His hand tightened on her waist.

'Weeks!' she amended with a rush. 'Days. Whenever you like. I love you, Rian. I swear it's only that. Once I was a little frightened of you . . . your dynamic aura . . . but not now. Never again!'

'Don't you believe it!' he said with hard mockery, and twisted her back in his arms, bending his dark head.

After a minute she broke away from him with a breathless little cry.

'Please, Rian!'

He laughed gently and took her hand, skirting the trees on their way back to the house.

A sickle moon rose above the lovely curve of the roof. The house was a dazzle of rose and gold lights from within the gleaming white façade washed by the pale radiance of moonlight.

'Belguardo!' Rian said, a vibrant note to his voice. 'My father once owned this land. It will most certainly belong to his grandson. I think that's rather fitting!'

Rory flushed a little and bent her head, but he tilted it up to him, claiming her life, her love, complete and absolute for his own.

'*Ubi bene ibi patria!*' he whispered in melodious Latin. 'Where the good land is, here is your country!'

His face suddenly swam before her eyes, her senses heightened unbearably, then he opened his arms and she went into them. Home.

THE THISTLE AND THE ROSE
by Margaret Rome

Helen considered that Damon, Marquis of Sanquhar, had treated
her young half-brother very shabbily, and she made up her mind
to get her own back on him. So when the opportunity presented
itself to work on his Scottish estate as his secretary, she jumped at
the opportunity. But she had underestimated the Marquis, and the
effect he was to have on her . . .

NOONFIRE
by Margaret Way

Rory's mother had brought her up to believe that all men were
ruthless, selfish and dangerous. Now Rory was alone, and the first
man to come into her life – the dynamic Rian McCallum – seemed
every bit as dangerous and dominating as her mother had declared.
And Rory was in no state to defend herself against him . . .

DARK VIKING
by Mary Wibberley

Emma was thrilled with her inheritance of a cottage in the
Shetland Islands, and would have loved every minute of her stay
there, if it hadn't been for her next-door neighbour, Greg Halcro.
For Greg was a man who got what he wanted – and he wanted
Emma to go away!

WILD INHERITANCE
by Margaret Pargeter

Alexa went to the West Coast of Scotland to take possession of a
croft that had been unexpectedly left to her by a distant relative.
But she met some opposition – from the mysterious Fergus, who
advised her against taking up residence; and from her neighbour,
Maxwell of Glenaird, who wanted her land and didn't seem to
have any qualms about taking her with it!

the rose of romance

How to join in a whole new world of romance

It's very easy to subscribe to the Mills & Boon Reader Service. As a regular reader, you can enjoy a whole range of special benefits. Bargain offers. Big cash savings. Your own free Reader Service newsletter, packed with knitting patterns, recipes, competitions, and exclusive book offers.

We send you the very latest titles each month, postage and packing free – no hidden extra charges. There's absolutely no commitment – you receive books for only as long as you want.

We'll send you details. Simply send the coupon – or drop us a line for details about the Mills & Boon Reader Service Subscription Scheme.
Post to: Mills & Boon Reader Service, P.O. Box 236, Thornton Road, Croydon, Surrey CR9 3RU, England.
*Please note: READERS IN SOUTH AFRICA please write to: Mills & Boon Reader Service of Southern Africa, Private Bag X3010, Randburg 2125, S. Africa.

Please send me details of the Mills & Boon Subscription Scheme.
NAME (Mrs/Miss) _____ EP3
ADDRESS _____

COUNTY/COUNTRY_____ POST/ZIP CODE_____
BLOCK LETTERS, PLEASE

Mills & Boon
the rose of romance